DEA

SCORPIO
(October 23 to November 21)

Scorpios are determined, sincere and courageous with tremendous personal magnetism. They appear strong-willed, but inside are tender and loving. Sincerity is the key to their relationships and they are never superficial. Scorpios need to discover what is going on beneath the surface and are not taken in by outward appearances - they have a deep understanding of people and life.

When Serena meets Matt, she senses a kindred spirit with whom she can bond. So when a car accident turns into something much more sinister, Sabrina is determined to help Matt - even though he is little more than a ghost.

ZODIAC

Whatever your sun sign, you'll want to read Zodiac, the series written in the stars.

ARIES (Mar 21 to Apr 19)   SECRET IDENTITY

TAURUS (Apr 20 to May 21)   BLACK OUT

GEMINI (May 22 to June 21)   MIRROR IMAGE

CANCER (Jun 22 to Jul 22)   DARK SHADOWS

LEO (Jul 23 to Aug 23)   STAGE FRIGHT

VIRGO (Aug 24 to Sep 23)   DESPERATELY YOURS

LIBRA (Sep 24 to Oct 22)   FROZEN IN TIME

SCORPIO (Oct 23 to Nov 21)   DEATH GRIP

SAGITTARIUS (Nov 22 to Dec 21)   STRANGE DESTINY

CAPRICORN (Dec 22 to Jan 19)   DON'T LOOK BACK

AQUARIUS (Jan 20 to Feb 19)   SECOND SIGHT

PISCES (Feb 20 to Mar 20)   SIXTH SENSE

SERIES CREATED BY JAHNNA N. MALCOLM

ZODIAC

SCORPIO

DEATH GRIP

JAHNNA N. MALCOLM

Lions

An Imprint of HarperCollins*Publishers*

First published in Lions in 1995
Lions is an imprint of CollinsChildren'sBooks,
a Division of HarperCollins*Publishers* Ltd,
77-85 Fulham Palace Road, Hammersmith, London W6 8JB

1 3 5 7 9 8 6 4 2

Copyright © Jahnna N. Malcolm 1995

The author asserts the moral right to be
identified as the author of the work

ISBN: 0 00 675055 9

Printed and bound in Great Britain by
HarperCollins Manufacturing Ltd, Glasgow.

Special Thanks to Jack Heifner

CHAPTER ONE

"Born on the cusp of Libra and Scorpio, you feel things intensely. Libra adds to your great appreciation of beauty but it is Scorpio in the eighth house that drives you."

"*T*he eighth house?" Sabrina Stallings whispered. She was seated across a round wooden table from an old woman in an Indian print skirt and blouse. The walls of the woman's shabby trailer were covered in richly patterned lengths of Asian fabric. A maroon and gold cotton print shawl with tasselled ends lay draped across the tiny couch filling one wall. The air was thick with the scent of burning oriental incense. "What does that mean?"

The grey-haired woman raised her head. Her eyes were clouded with cataracts but her face was lit with the expression of one who sees far beyond the range of human sight. "The eighth house is the mystic life force. It represents birth, passionate love – and death."

"Death?" Sabrina swallowed hard. She'd had enough of death in her life. First her grandparents, one from illness, the other from heartbreak. Then her mother from cancer. Now it was just Sabrina and her father, facing the world alone.

The old woman nodded. "Yes. The Mayans called Scorpio the death-god." She lifted a misshapen finger, bent with arthritis. "But remember – with death comes rebirth. As it ever was, after winter comes spring."

No spring had followed Sabrina's winter. Ever since her mother's death nearly twelve months before, Sabrina had felt nothing but a gaping, hollow sorrow.

The old woman nodded, as if reading Sabrina's thoughts. "Saturn in Virgo in the seventh house can make you secretive, grave, and somewhat melancholy. You approach everything you do with a fierce intensity – even grieving."

Sabrina shivered. How could this woman know? Maybe it was the way she dressed these days. Black from head to toe – long skirt, black turtleneck and waistcoat – even black lace-up boots. Even her hair was jet black, styled in a short china-doll cut. Her father said that in all of those black clothes she reminded him of a character from Chekhov's play, *The Seagull*. Masha, who always wore black because she was "in mourning for her life". And that's how Sabrina often felt. In mourning for everything.

"Your Moon is in Taurus in the third house, which is ruled by Mercury," Madame Zoaunne continued. "You have an active and inquisitive mind. I see travel and many journeys in your chart."

"That's incredible," Sabrina gasped. "My family has done nothing but travel since I was born. I just moved to Innisfree from Sri Lanka."

Madame Zoaunne raised her head. "There are many types of journeys, spiritually as well as physically. Because Neptune is in Aquarius in the twelfth house, you are extremely mystical and will travel many roads in your life. You have great intuition and perception, often seeing what others do not."

The old astrologer cocked her head at Sabrina, as if to say "Am I right?"

Sabrina did see and feel things that other people, like her father and friends, seemed to miss. She had the ability to walk into a room and know who was happy, who held great sadness, and who would be the source of a problem before the day was out. "I used to feel that I wasn't alone," she murmured to the old woman.

Madame Zoaunne nodded. "Many spirits walk this earth. Some of us know when they are with us."

Because of her family's travelling, Sabrina had spent much time by herself and had taken comfort in those moments when she felt "others" were in the room. "When I was little, I called them my guardian angels."

The old woman smiled, revealing several craggy nicotine stained teeth. "Wherever there is love, there is an angel nearby." Then she nodded pleasantly over her shoulder as if she were sharing her joke with others in the room.

Just as quickly the woman frowned back at the chart. "It is important that you stay connected to these caretaker spirits because your chart – with Venus in Libra in the eighth house and Mars in Gemini in the fourth house makes your life filled with inharmonies. I see possible accidents, possible loss, and a legacy connected with death."

"Does this mean I'm going to die soon?" Sabrina asked boldly. She was never one to flinch in the face of bad news. She'd faced it so often.

"Oh my, no," the woman replied. "It means nothing of the sort. But because your horoscope is tipped it puts Pisces in the first house where Aries should normally be. That means that you are a more malleable person. More acted upon than acting. Things will happen to you. Pluto is in Aquarius in the twelfth house, which also indicates explosive endings and beginnings to all the phases of your life."

Sabrina slumped back in her chair. For her birthday her father had given her a visit to this astrologer. She'd looked forward to the visit, hoping to hear good news about their move and her life. But all this woman talked about was death. *Which I've had enough of.*

The kettle resting on a hot plate behind Madame Zoaunne began to whistle. "Would you care for a cup of Darjeeling?" the astrologer asked. "I see you could probably use one."

"Thanks, I could probably drink a gallon of it." Sabrina had become a big tea drinker. And coffee. She loved intense cups of thick, black, hot coffee.

As the old woman moved to make them both a cup, Sabrina said, "My chart seems pretty dreary."

"Dreary?" Madame Zoaunne gasped as the water splattered over the side of the cup, making little steaming sounds as it hit the cold porcelain sink. "Your chart is nothing short of remarkable. Here, sip your tea and I will explain more."

Sabrina took the flowered teacup and sank comfortably into the soft cushion on the large round rattan chair. It rested on a rattan pedestal and was called a *mama san*, just perfect for curling up in with a good book.

The astrologer set her cup down and smoothed her hand across the astrological chart she had drawn for Sabrina. She had called it her ephemeris. The chart was a large map with a circle in its centre. The circle was divided into twelve sections, each representing one of the twelve houses of the zodiac. Little symbols that looked like Chinese characters had been carefully drawn in each house. There were moons and *m*'s written with an arrow through them. And something that looked like a pitchfork. There were also the familiar male and female symbols of a circle with an arrow, and a circle with a cross.

"First of all, I must stress that you are

extremely connected to the mystical world," Madame Zoaunne explained. "Your psychic powers allow you to experience things on a different level from the average person."

So far the only level Sabrina had experienced was the lower level of absolute depression.

"Now, you mustn't despair. Jupiter is in Cancer in the fifth house. This shows great success in connection with school and life."

Sabrina put her cup back on her saucer and sighed. "Well, that's good news. I'm just starting at a new school on Monday."

The woman raised an eyebrow. "You will be extremely popular and make many friends. Uranus is in Capricorn, which indicates that these new friends will be very unusual people. Eccentric friends who will come in and out of your lives."

"Lives?" Sabrina repeated. "As in more than one life?"

"But of course," Madame Zoaunne shrugged. "You think one little life is enough? Not for me. Certainly not for you."

Sabrina took another sip of her tea, trying to absorb Madame Zoaunne's words. Then she asked the question she'd been dying to ask since she'd arrived.

"Do you see any romance in my chart?" Sabrina asked, peering at the old lady over her cup of tea. She had travelled to many places, had a number of interesting friends, but had never really fallen in love. She ached for a great romance.

"Love covers your chart," Madame Zoaunne said, sweeping her hand over the paper. "See here? Uranus is opposing Jupiter from the eleventh to fifth houses. You love Love. You are liable to fall in love suddenly with a friend and it will be *big*." The woman waved both hands. "Monumental. I told you, Sabrina, you are a powerhouse of emotional energy. Love for you is intense, spiritual and passionate."

Sabrina smiled for the first time since her reading with Madame Zoaunne had begun. "Will it come soon?"

The old woman scanned her daily charts and gasped, putting her hand to her chest. "No wonder you are not seeing the beauty in life. Venus is retrograde. This aspect can be very stressful. You want love, and it is out there reaching for you – but you are afraid."

Sabrina nodded.

"It is there, but you have been too guarded, too cautious. Open your heart," the old woman said softly. "For a great love is your destiny, Sabrina. Your destiny."

CHAPTER TWO

SCORPIO (October 23 - November 21)
Current aspects bring adventure and romance
into your life, but also a challenge of some
kind. Emotional? Mental? Try not to be
pessimistic. You Scorpios can handle it all.

New beginnings are good, Sabrina told herself over and over again that October morning. She tried desperately to believe her own words. When she tugged on the heavy wooden and bevelled glass door to Innisfree High School and hurried inside, the skin on her arms immediately broke out into tiny goose bumps.

Why is it so cold? The crumbling red brick building looked far too old to be air-conditioned. Perhaps it was the worn deep blue tile floor and gunmetal grey lockers that made the main hallway feel thirty degrees cooler than the warm autumn day outside.

No. Sabrina knew that it always felt that way

in this school. Chilly. Except how could she know that? Sabrina had never been in this building before.

She closed her eyes and did what she always did in a new place – tried to feel the vibrations. At first, what Sabrina felt was good. Yes, she was happy to finally be back in the United States, in this quiet, picturesque town on the Northern California coast.

Sure, it would be difficult to adjust but when had she ever backed away from trying anything new? Following her parents in their travels round the globe, Sabrina had learned to deal with language barriers, strange customs and extremely varied living conditions. The teenagers in Innisfree couldn't be any harder to get to know than kids from round the world. Could they?

New beginnings are good, she repeated to herself like a mantra. *They just have to be.*

Ouch! Suddenly, pain like a dagger stabbed into Sabrina's skull. Her hand flew to the back of her neck, half expecting to pull out a knife or, at least, swat some venomous insect. Nothing was there.

But as much as Sabrina tried to let positive thoughts rule the moment, her intuitive powers continued to send out one alarming, contradictory message. *Something is really, terribly wrong in this place.*

Sensing she was no longer alone in the strange, yet familiar, hallway, Sabrina opened her eyes to see a few students wandering the icy corridor. Why were all of them looking her way – studying her as if she was a strange new species from another world? *I'll stare right back!*

Bam!

A door under a sign reading SCHOOL OFFICE flew open and slammed into the wall, making Sabrina nearly jump out of her skin. A blonde in a cheerleading outfit rushed into the hallway, then stopped and turned in a circle, as if looking for something, or somebody.

In a flash another girl, with long dark hair, ran from an adjoining doorway and grabbed the blonde by the shoulders. Then the two whispered together. The dark-haired girl seemed pleased about something.

Could that be where the darkness was coming from? From the two girls who seemed to be hatching a plot or planning some secret act? *No.*

At that moment the girls turned and stared

hard at Sabrina. They whispered once more, then hurried down the hallway. They looked back at Sabrina one last time before disappearing into another corridor.

So much for Madame Zoaunne's prediction that I would make lots of friends. Maybe it's my clothes.

Sabrina was wearing her usual uniform of black. Today it was a leather skirt, with a black linen collarless shirt, black tights, and lace-up boots. In an attempt to add some colour, she'd put a crimson beret on top of her chin-length raven hair and outlined her large green eyes a little more heavily than usual. Finally, she'd chosen a vibrant scarlet lipstick. Red and black were considered lucky for Scorpios. She had hoped the combination would be lucky for her.

The hall seemed completely empty and yet Sabrina felt there was still someone there. Turning round, she caught a glimpse of a figure sneaking up the stairway to the second floor. It appeared to be a short boy with black hair, wearing a dark T-shirt and baggy shorts. Or maybe it was a girl. Or a phantom.

"One of Madame Zoaunne's caretaker spirits," Sabrina murmured out loud. Footsteps echoed until the sounds faded into silence. "I guess not."

Again, she was alone – or thought she was until a hand grabbed her elbow.

"Oh!" Sabrina let out a small gasp as a jolt of electricity shot up her arm.

A male voice behind her asked, "Lost?"

Sabrina spun and found herself staring into the pale blue eyes of an extremely handsome, very tanned boy. His slightly crooked smile, which seemed to curve up a little higher on one side than the other, gave her the first warm feeling she'd had since entering this strange new world.

"Who, me, lost? Never!" Sabrina declared with a toss of her head.

The boy continued to stare at her, amused. His honey coloured hair, which touched his shoulders, was pushed casually behind his ears, exposing a small gold hoop earring on the left side.

Sabrina shrugged. "OK, maybe a little bit lost. Actually, I was trying to get a feel for the place."

"Checking the vibes?" His eyes were still locked with hers.

Sabrina nodded, mesmerized by the tiny flecks of gold that highlighted his pale blue eyes. "I believe that people and places have good and bad vibrations. You can tell a lot about them by simply closing your eyes and letting yourself feel those vibes."

"So, what can you tell about me?" he asked, continuing to smile.

Sabrina closed her eyes. *That you have a smile and personality that could melt icecaps*, was what she thought. "That you are warm and open," was what she said.

"That's all?" The boy looked a bit disappointed and his smile faded into a tiny pout. "My dog is warm and open. Can't you sense anything else?"

"Let me think." Sabrina tapped her finger to her lips and then walked in a slow circle round the boy, sizing him up. He wore a navy-blue cardigan sweater, left unbuttoned, with a large A on the front. Underneath, his white T-shirt was pulled tightly across his muscular chest.

His faded jeans weren't too baggy or too tight, and he wore black running shoes. As Sabrina circled he looked slightly uncomfortable, feeling as if he was on display. "Time's up," he announced finally.

Sabrina, who had enjoyed being in control, took a long pause before she announced her verdict. "OK, here goes. I can also tell you're an outgoing kind of person, probably on the student council. You like team sports, but not so much that they take over your life. You're well-rounded, like to read great books and, along with everyone else, read the comics first in the newspaper. Am I right?" She opened her arms, waiting to see if she'd got the profile correct.

He laughed, causing a lock of his blond hair to fall over his forehead. He pushed it back absently with his hand. "How could you know all that? You're not some kind of witch, are you?"

Sabrina leant forward and whispered, "Of course I'm a witch. All Scorpios have a line to the occult. However, at the moment I am simply using my mortal powers of observation." She pointed to his sweater. "That is a letter sweater, so you're into sports. Your notebook has a tab in it labelled, 'Student Council Projects'. You've got Ray Bradbury's *Dandelion Wine* tucked into your sweater pocket, which by the way happens to be one of my favourite books. And I guessed the last part about the comics."

"Brilliant!" He was clearly enjoying their exchange and the smile quickly returned to his face. "I possess a few magical powers myself."

"You do?" Sabrina folded her arms across her chest. "Then tell me what you know about me."

Now it was his turn to circle round Sabrina. He made one complete revolution before speaking. "You like black."

Sabrina rolled her eyes. "What was your first clue, Sherlock?"

"Not because you look good in it – which by the way you do. But because it reflects the way you view the world," he added, never taking his eyes off her face.

"Go on." This was fun, this curious meeting dance they were doing.

"You like music," he announced firmly.

"Do you know anybody our age who doesn't?" Sabrina pulled a Walkman and headphones out of her leather shoulder bag to illustrate.

"You like to read," he continued. "Enough to say 'one of my favourite books' implying, of course, that *Dandelion Wine* is just one of many that you have read." He was getting into the game now. "You are open, direct, and must be used to travel or moving because you're not shy at all. And you've just come from another country, or I guess I should say, have been living in another country." He stopped circling and waited for her response.

Sabrina paused, letting him wonder a bit as to whether his guesses were correct. Frankly, she was a bit amazed that he'd read her so correctly. Then she smiled. "My father and I have just moved back to the States from Sri Lanka. It's an island in the—"

"Indian Ocean," he cut in, completing her sentence. "It was once known as Ceylon."

He's smart, although he's a bit too pleased with himself at the moment.

"I'm not as smart as you might think," he said, as if he had just read her mind. This unnerved Sabrina a bit. "I happen to love geography – oceanography, actually – because I surf. I can't say the same thing about calculus."

"How did you know I was from a foreign country?"

He pointed to her bag. "When you pulled out your Walkman, I saw a passport. Nobody casually carries a passport unless they've been living somewhere where it was necessary."

"Well, you're correct on all counts," Sabrina said.

"How come you're in Innisfree?" he continued. "Seems to me someone who has lived all over the world would find this place terminally dull."

"My father is a photo-journalist, and he and my mother always liked Northern California. He's writing a novel and needed to come back to the States and live somewhere quiet...so here we are."

"Well, it's certainly quiet in Innisfree. Too quiet." He grinned again and there was silence as he and Sabrina looked at one another.

I like him. A lot. I wonder if he can tell. Sabrina smiled in answer to her own question. *Of course he can tell.*

Brrring! The school bell burst through Sabrina's thoughts, reminding her what she was really there for. "School! I haven't even registered for classes."

Sabrina made a move towards the school office when the boy darted in front of her. "Hey, you can't go. I don't even know your name."

"Sabrina Stallings." She stuck out her hand. "What's yours?"

"Matt Pierce." He took her hand in between both of his. "Welcome to Innisfree."

His touch sent another charge of electricity through her. "Thanks for talking to me," she said. "I was beginning to think I had two heads or something."

"No, just one pretty one."

You are a flirt!

"Oh, and it's a pretty name, Sabrina."

"My father had a thing for Audrey Hepburn when he was our age," she explained. "She once starred in a movie called *Sabrina*—"

"—*Fair*. With Humphrey Bogart." Again, Matt finished her sentence.

Sabrina was amazed, since she'd never met any boy her age who knew that piece of movie trivia. But for all her apparent sophistication, Sabrina hadn't really had too many dates.

"Are you a movie fan, Matt?" She liked saying his name.

Matt nodded. "Especially old ones. I'm sure you've been told you kind of look like Audrey Hepburn. Dark hair, big eyes, skinny..."

Skinny? Sabrina started to protest, but they were no longer alone. The once empty hallway was filled with students heading to classes.

From behind, a loud voice yelled in their direction. "Matt, have you seen Jeff?"

Sabrina looked back and spotted an attractive redhead hurrying towards them. She wore a short plaid skirt, white blouse and waistcoat, and green Doc Martens.

"Haven't seen Jeff all morning," Matt replied, shaking his head. "Sabrina Stallings, meet Heather Deemer. This is Sabrina's first day at Innisfree High."

"Uh, oh. The other girls aren't going to like you," Heather said, with a slight grimace. "*Major* competition."

"Oh?" Sabrina took that as a compliment. *A weird compliment.*

"We're having a dance on Saturday," Heather continued. "I'm on the decoration committee and as usual no one's shown up. If you want to come, we're meeting after school in the gym. You might be able to meet people. We're desperate."

"Thanks, Heather." *I think.*

Heather turned her focus back to Matt. "I'm worried about Jeff. He promised to meet me on the steps before my Spanish class." She nervously chewed on her lower lip. "I guess I'd better keep looking. See you later." With that, Heather hurried down the hallway.

Matt watched her go and shook his head. "I hate to break it to her but Jeff is probably escorting some sophomore to class. The guy can be a real slime."

"Matt, code blue!" A boy's head suddenly

popped between them, causing Matt and Sabrina to jump apart.

The boy was very tall and very thin, with light red hair in a crew cut. He was wearing wire-rimmed glasses, black chinos, a white shirt, skinny tie and black hightop sneakers.

"Geez, Oz, you scared us half to death," Matt croaked.

"Sorry, buddy," the boy said, "but I'm having a total meltdown."

Matt put his hand on the boy's arm. "Before you do, take a deep breath and say hello to Sabrina Stallings. She's new."

The boy sucked in a big breath of air and held it. Turning to Sabrina, he squeaked, "Pleased to meet you. I'm Osgood Horton."

"Oz for short," Matt said, slapping him on the back.

Oz exhaled loudly. "I'm sorry. But Innisfree High has just been declared a disaster area. I just got back my SAT scores and they're too low. Do you understand what that means?" He put his face near Sabrina's. "This could have catastrophic effects."

Sabrina tried to console him. "I've heard that test scores don't really measure a person's intelligence. Often the people who score high are really only good at taking tests."

"Right! And I am one of those people," Oz replied, jabbing his chest with his thumb. "I'm the king of test takers."

"Osgood was declared a genius at the age of five," Matt explained.

"I've tested 100% all through school," Osgood added. "I have a straight A average. I can do the *New York Times* crossword puzzle in less than five minutes—"

"In ink!" Matt cut in.

"And—" Osgood's face grew redder and redder. "I never, *ever* blow tests!"

"Hey, calm down, before you blow a fuse!" Matt patted Oz on the back. "Obviously there's been a mistake. You simply tell the office and they'll straighten things out."

Oz adjusted his glasses. "I don't trust those guys," he muttered. "They don't understand it's my future they've screwed up."

"How do you see your future?" Sabrina asked as she studied this very odd boy. She wondered if he was one of the people Madame Zoaunne had referred to. He certainly qualified as a unique individual.

"I've had my future planned since I was ten." Oz ticked off his list on his fingers.

"Undergraduate work, MIT. MBA, Harvard Business School. President of a large multinational corporation by the age of thirty."

"Not of the United States?" Matt raised an eyebrow.

Oz winced. "No way. That job is for all-American-loved-by-all guys like you."

"Believe me, I don't want to be president either." Matt shuddered. "Who'd want that kind of pressure? Ugh."

"So what do you see yourself doing in the future, Matt?" Sabrina asked.

Matt cocked his head and thought a moment. "I'm really not sure what I want to do. I used to see myself as an astronaut, then maybe as some sort of Jacques Cousteau type. Now I don't know. The future seems like a very grey area." He grinned at her. "What are you going to do? Maybe we could do it together?"

Brrring! Before Sabrina could come up with a clever answer, the bell saved her once more.

"That's the second bell. We'd better get to class," exclaimed Oz. "Metcalfe deducts tardy points from the grade. Have to keep up my points, you know." Osgood immediately took off down the hallway towards the far end of the corridor, his long legs covering the distance in half the time it would have taken a normal sized person.

"And I'd better find the office and register," Sabrina sighed. She wasn't anxious to part from Matt. She was starting to feel very attached to him.

"Hey, I wish I could take you in there," Matt said with a shrug, "but I've gotta get to Metcalfe's class, too. Not because of my points," he added ruefully, "but because I *don't* have any! The office is over there." He gestured towards the big wooden door to their left, the same one the hysterical blonde girl had run through earlier.

"Thanks. See you later, maybe?" Sabrina asked, hopefully.

Matt shook his hair out of his eyes and then rested his hand on her shoulder. "Yes, you will," he said earnestly. "Saturday, eight o'clock, at the dance."

"What?" Sabrina blinked in surprise.

"Didn't I tell you?" Matt laughed. "That's your destiny – to be my date for the dance." With that he winked, then turned and jogged towards the classroom door.

"My destiny," Sabrina murmured, watching him go. Those had been Madame Zoaunne's words exactly. For the first time in a year the future held the promise of hope. Sabrina flung open the door to the school office and announced to the startled secretary, "I'm Sabrina Stallings. You don't know me yet, but you will."

CHAPTER THREE

*Dazzle and diplomacy are what you're all
about. Even though your feelings may
sometimes get a little intense, you'll soon put
things back into balance. Wobbly Neptune in
Pisces whispers of the occult.
Listen to those voices.*

Whoosh! A steady rain pelted the windscreen
of the car, making it difficult for Sabrina's
father to see where he was driving. His mind,
however, was not completely on the road.

"I still don't understand why your date didn't
come to fetch you," Mr Stallings grumbled.
"That way I could have met him."

Sabrina's father had been out of the States for
so long that he seemed a bit old-fashioned for
someone only in his mid-forties. Still, Sabrina
thought he was very handsome, with his salt-
and-pepper hair and matching beard.

"I told you, Dad, Matt's car is in the garage.

And besides, we agreed to meet at the dance. It was my suggestion."

Sabrina had spent the week falling head over heels in love with Matt. Usually she kept her focus fixed solidly on work and school. But, from the moment they'd met, all Sabrina could think about was when she'd be able to see Matt again.

"Why would you suggest that?" her father asked, stroking his neatly trimmed beard. "Don't girls like to be courted any more?"

Because things are moving too fast, was what Sabrina thought. What she said was, "This makes everything more casual."

That explanation seemed to satisfy her father. "Casual is good," he nodded appreciatively. "Kids today seem to rush headlong into everything."

Her father turned his full attention back on the rain-soaked road before them, while Sabrina relaxed in her seat and daydreamed of Matt. Madame Zoaunne couldn't have been more right. Love had come into Sabrina's life like an explosion of fireworks. Matt was more than just a handsome boy. He seemed to be the puzzle piece that made her complete, like one of those valentine necklaces with two pieces that lock together to form a perfect heart. Matt made Sabrina happy. And happiness, with all of its silly, giggling, bubbly sides, was what Sabrina had been missing for so much of her life.

"Careful!" Sabrina exclaimed as her father swerved to miss a fallen branch. The road was slippery and the car skidded sideways. As Sabrina clutched the dashboard, the other, more disturbing things the astrologer had told her, about accidents, loss and death, flashed through her mind.

"Are you OK?" her father asked, when the car had straightened back out.

Sabrina nodded stiffly. "I think so. But that scared me a bit."

Her father gripped the wheel a little tighter and leant forward, peering intently through the rain-streaked windscreen. "This is a terrible night for anyone to be out," he murmured. "Maybe we should just go home."

"Dad!" Sabrina gasped.

"Well, you said this date was casual," her father said, shooting a glance her way.

"Not *that* casual," Sabrina replied. "Don't worry. The dance is inside the gym. I won't get wet."

Sabrina spied the lights of the school ahead

and her stomach did a strange flip-flop. That uneasy feeling, the one she'd had when she first stepped in the school, still lingered. As if something terrible was about to happen. Maybe not to her but to someone close to her. Sabrina clutched her stomach.

Her father saw her movement and frowned. "Hey, if you're not feeling well, you don't have to go. We can find this boy and call off the date."

"Dad!" Sabrina whispered. "Please be careful driving home. You're not really used to this car." In Sri Lanka he'd become accustomed to handling an old, dented Rover, not this large American road warrior.

"I'll be careful, I promise." Her father reached over and squeezed her hand. "You too?"

Sabrina smiled. "Promise."

Mr Stallings turned the car into the parking lot by the gymnasium. "This must be the place." He rolled down the car window and stuck his head out to look at the gym. "What luck! I think the rain is stopping."

"Good!" Sabrina was happy not to get her dress wet. It was a long-sleeved black knit dress that hugged her figure. She wore the colourful, dangly earrings her mother had given her just before she died.

Sabrina kissed her father on the cheek. "Matt said if I got myself here, he would get me home. I'll see you later. And before you say it – no, I won't be late."

She opened the door to the car and got out, then leant back inside for one last comment. "When I get home you'd better be asleep," Sabrina scolded teasingly. "I don't want to hear you say you stayed up working on your book, when you were really up worrying about me."

Her dad laughed. "Have a good time. You look beautiful and I'm proud of you."

"Proud of me? What for?"

"For following your mom and me all over the world and never complaining once. I know it's a little difficult fitting in here. Especially when you're not your typical American girl."

Sabrina put her hands on her hips. "I have absolutely no desire to be typical, thank you very much. I'm aiming for something more along the lines of remarkable."

Her father chuckled. "That you are, my dear. That you are."

Sabrina closed the car door and dashed up the steps to the school. She could feel the thumping bass in her feet as she flung open the door. The sound of a screeching guitar assaulted her but that wasn't why she gasped in alarm.

That terrible foreboding feeling cut through her like a knife. Sabrina paused, waiting for it to pass. And then she stepped into the gymnasium. *I'm going to have a good time tonight. Or else.*

The huge, vaulted space was dark, but Sabrina could successfully make out the shapes of couples dancing together. Orange, yellow and red balloons floated above the highly polished hardwood floor.

Maybe she should have helped Heather with the decorations, but Sabrina would have wanted to do something more inventive. Balloons were so expected and not terribly thrilling to anyone over the age of ten. They certainly were not her style. Granted, orange, yellow and red were autumn colours, but there simply had to be something more exciting than balloons and crepe paper!

"Do you have a ticket? I'll sell you one if you don't."

Sabrina blinked in the direction of the voice. Her eyes started to adjust to the dim light and she saw Jodi Biggs heading her way. Jodi was a cute, blonde cheerleader that Matt had introduced her to midweek. She seemed to have a bubbly personality. Perhaps a bit too bubbly at the moment. Still, she had been nice to Sabrina.

Jodi appeared to be weaving a little as she walked. As she got closer, Sabrina was surprised to hear Jodi slurring her words. Her breath smelled of alcohol.

"Someone should have told you, we don't dress up for our dances." Jodi's outfit confirmed this. She was wearing a pair of jeans and a "No Fear" sweatshirt. "There's a big pile of shoes over there, if you want to dump yours."

Sabrina looked down at her black heels. "Uh, no thanks."

"Your ticket?" Jodi stuck out her hand. The movement threw her off balance and she clutched the table holding the cash box, trying to steady herself.

Matt had bought a ticket for Sabrina on Friday and she'd tucked it into her small shoulder bag. Sabrina handed the ticket to Jodi, who squinted at it, swaying.

"Is everything all right?" Sabrina bent forward to peer in Jodi's face.

Jodi looked up from the ticket. "There's writing on the back."

"Oh, that!" Sabrina giggled. "Matt wrote

that."

Jodi's face visibly drooped as she read out loud, "Cinderella, see you at the ball! Fairy Godmother has arranged for a full moon. Should be a perfect night for Happily Ever Aftering. Love, Prince C. P.S. Don't forget the glass slippers."

Sabrina was glad the gym was dark because she could feel her face turning a bright red. "Is it all right if I keep that?" she asked. "As a memento."

Jodi squinted up at Sabrina. "No. You can't. We need the tickets for the head count." With that she stuffed the ticket into the change box and slammed the lid.

Anxious to get as far away from the tipsy girl as possible, Sabrina moved into the darkness at the edge of the dance floor.

"Stop it, Jeff," Heather Deemer's voice shouted over the music. She and Jeff Winstead were dancing in front of Sabrina. Jeff was a handsome guy, with dark curly hair and a powerful build. He wore torn jeans and a T-shirt that had "Harley-Davidson" printed on it.

It had only taken one or two brief exchanges with Jeff for Sabrina to decide that he didn't have a lot going for him in the brains department. But he seemed nice enough.

Although the music was blaring so loudly that Sabrina couldn't hear their conversation, it was clear that the couple were definitely having some sort of argument. Without warning, Heather slapped Jeff across the cheek. Then she broke into tears and ran towards the girls' restroom.

Jeff looked stunned as he spun in a circle with his arms spread wide. "What did I do?" he demanded of anyone who would look in his direction. When no one responded, he stormed off in the opposite direction, a murderous look on his face.

Suddenly a hand slid along her waist and a low voice murmured in her ear. "Enjoying the floor show?"

Sabrina felt her entire body tingling. This was really the first physical contact she'd had with Matt, and it felt wonderful.

"You look fantastic," he whispered, nuzzling her ear.

Sabrina turned to face Matt. He wore a denim shirt, jeans, and cowboy boots. "So do you."

The music shifted to a slow dance and Matt placed both hands on Sabrina's waist. Slowly they started rocking back in forth in time to the music.

"Well, Sabrina, you move fast." Blair Stratton, one of the first people Sabrina had seen at Innisfree High, suddenly appeared beside them.

Sabrina opened her mouth to reply but Matt spoke for her. "I like fast," he said.

"I didn't even know you two knew each other," Blair continued.

"Sabrina's my soul mate," Matt replied, not taking his eyes off Sabrina.

Blair laughed. "Matt, you can be so melodramatic." She nudged Sabrina. "When we were going together he used to say things like that all the time."

"That's a lie, Blair," Matt said, good-naturedly. "And you know it."

Blair was Innisfree's resident beauty. Her hair was black and she wore it long, down to her shoulders.

Unlike the others at the dance, Blair was not dressed casually. She wore a turquoise lycra mini-dress.

"Look, Matt, my date doesn't arrive from Stanford until later," Blair said. "But you know how much I like to dance. Will you dance the next one with me? Just for old time's sake."

"Sorry, Blair. I've reserved every dance for Sabrina." Matt wrapped his arms round Sabrina's waist, pulling her even closer to him. "Go and ask Jeff. He seems to be missing a partner."

"Jeff?" Blair scoffed. "Get real." Then she turned on her heel and strode off.

Sabrina raised an eyebrow at Matt. "Are all your old girlfriends that charming?"

"Ignore Blair," Matt murmured, spinning Sabrina to the centre of the dance floor. "She can't stand competition. She'll just have to get over it."

"I hope so." Sabrina wrapped her arms round Matt's neck and rested her cheek on his shoulder. No words were spoken as one slow song melted into another.

They danced like that for a full half-hour, until Jodi, even tipsier than before, interrupted them.

"Hey, Sabrina," she mumbled, watery-eyed. "You're my friend. Will you help me find my date? I don't see him anywhere."

Sabrina touched Jodi's arm and spoke in a quiet voice. "Jodi, you look like you're not feeling well. Maybe you'd better sit down for a while."

"I don't want to sit! I want someone to dance with me!" With that Jodi stomped off, weaving her way through a row of chairs inhabited by a few lonely-looking boys and girls, all too shy to ask each other to dance.

"What's with everyone tonight?" Matt murmured. "It must be the moon, they've all turned into werewolves."

Sabrina agreed. "There do seem to be a lot of unhappy people here tonight."

Matt pulled away to look in her eyes. "You may not believe this, but this is not normal. Generally, the kids at IHS are pretty cool."

Over Matt's shoulder, Sabrina watched Jodi stumble back to the table where tickets had been taken, slip something into her jacket and stagger to the back door of the gym. At the door Jodi paused and defiantly met Sabrina's gaze. Then she disappeared into the night.

There was a short break in the music. Matt guided Sabrina towards the refreshment table. "Let's get something to drink."

"Sounds good to me," Sabrina said. "I'm parched."

"Students of Innisfree, unite," a voice suddenly blasted over the PA system.

44

Sabrina looked back at the stage. Osgood, looking in much the same condition as Jodi, stood swaying in front of the microphone. "I am Oz, the great and powerful," he joked, imitating lines from the Wizard of Oz.

"Pay no attention to the geek behind the microphone," someone joked back at him.

"No, really!" Osgood held up his hands to stop the laughter coming from the crowd on the dance floor. "I'm doing a small survey here. How many of you who took the SAT tests feel you were cheated? Given a rotten score."

Sabrina was surprised to see a great many hands shoot up.

"Good." Osgood staggered backwards, poking at the centre of his glasses with one finger. He approached the microphone again. "Tonight I'm announcing the Osgood Challenge. If all of us band together to protest those scores, then the school will retest everyone."

"Why don't you just retake the test?" Jeff Winstead shouted from the back. He was standing next to Mandy Gibbs, a cute sophomore in Sabrina's French class. "One time was enough for me! Now get off the stage — we want to hear some music."

"No. Don't you see?" Osgood was too close to the microphone and it emitted a high-pitched squeal, causing everyone to cover their ears. "If I retake it and get a great score – which is what will happen – they'll just say I was having a bad day the first time round. But I want them to admit they made a mistake."

Many of the kids on the floor didn't care about the test since they weren't planning on going to college or, like Jeff, they planned on sailing in on athletic scholarships. But it was essential that Osgood got an academic scholarship. Besides needing the money, his pride was at stake. "Aw, come on, you guys." Osgood was now starting to whine. "This is important."

"To whom?" Blair Stratton called. She had moved to the foot of the stage and was trying to coax Oz to stop. "Come on, Oz, drop it, will you? Nobody cares."

This only made Osgood more adamant. He grabbed the mike, setting off another round of ear-splitting squeals of feedback. "Listen. Monday we march on the principal's office."

Blair was now leading the chant, "Start the music! Get off the stage!" The chant became louder and louder as more and more students joined in.

Matt turned to Sabrina. "I'd better get Oz outta here before the teachers throw him out. They'll report that he's been drinking and he'll be in major trouble."

"I'll go with you." Sabrina and Matt made their way towards the stage, pushing through the angry crowd that was growing more and more restless. "Get off the stage! We want music!" It was beginning to sound like a chant at a football game.

"Oz, give me your car keys." Matt said matter-of-factly, hopping up on the stage next to Osgood. "It's time to go."

"We can't go now." Oz gestured clumsily at the crowd. "These guys are getting really angry."

"Yeah," Matt said, looping his arm through his friend's elbow. "At you. Now give me your keys. We're going home."

Matt was firm in his command, so Oz reached in his pocket, fished out the keys and tossed them to Matt.

Sabrina took Osgood's other arm as Matt led him off the stage. She said to Matt. "You go get the car and I'll wait here with Oz.

Oz locked his knees and folded his arms

stubbornly across his chest. "I'm not leaving."

"All right." Sabrina threw her hands in the air. "Be that way. But when Mr Gordon, who just happens to be walking this way, reports to the principal that you have been drinking, and they don't even let you retake that test, don't say I didn't warn you."

"Mr Gordon?" Oz suddenly grabbed Sabrina's arm. "Get me out of here," he whispered. "Quick."

Sabrina guided him towards the exit. As she did, Oz whimpered, "I want you to know, Sabrina, that I never, ever drink. I've just been so upset about my test scores, I think I'm losing it."

As they left the gym, Sabrina was acutely aware that several students were watching her. Blair and Heather were huddled together, whispering.

Then Sabrina saw something that unnerved her completely. The strange boy with the dyed black hair had slipped out of the door after her and was now creeping along behind them in the shadows.

Matt drove Osgood's car up to the kerb at the back. It was an old Buick that had been in so many wrecks that it really didn't have any shape or colour left. It was just a blend of pale green, grey and rust.

"We're going to take you home, Oz," Sabrina murmured to the half-conscious boy. "And I guarantee that things will look a lot better tomorrow."

"Really?" Osgood looked down at Sabrina with watery eyes. "You promise?"

Sabrina opened her mouth to promise, but something stopped her. Just thinking about tomorrow made her insides do a flip-flop. In the meanwhile, Matt had jumped out of the front seat and struggled to tuck Osgood into the back seat. It was tough, but together they managed to squeeze Oz's long legs in and close the door.

This entire scene was repeated in reverse at Oz's house, as they did their best to get him up to the front porch without waking anyone. Sabrina waited outside as Matt slipped Osgood in and put him to bed. Five minutes later, Matt reappeared.

"Is he asleep?" Sabrina whispered as she got up from the porch swing. Matt nodded and the two of them tiptoed down the steps and hurried towards Osgood's car.

"His little brother woke up and I had to pay him a dollar to buy his silence, but I think Oz

49

will sleep it off." Matt chuckled quietly as he opened the car's front door for Sabrina to get in. Then he hurried round to the driver's side.

"Is it OK that you take Oz's car?" Sabrina asked as he started the car and drove away.

"Sure, he trusts me. Besides, I promised I'd take you home. This is the only way, unless we walk, and it looks like the rain is going to start again. Any objection?" He turned to her and smiled.

"No. Are we going home?" Sabrina asked.

"We can go back to the dance. It's still early," he said as they pulled into the school parking lot. He stopped the car but kept the engine running. "Or I can you show you the prettiest spot in Innisfree. Your choice."

Matt's eyes twinkled mischievously and Sabrina couldn't help laughing. "Some choice. A dreary dance filled with too many jealous ex-girlfriends. Or the prettiest spot in Innisfree. I'll take a chance. Show me this spot."

"Your wish is my command." Matt pulled away from the kerb a little too fast, causing the tyres to spin on the wet road. As a heavy rain began to fall, Matt guided the old Buick towards the ocean.

CHAPTER FOUR

*T*he winding road led away from Innisfree up into the rugged mountains south of town. Tucked inside Osgood's old Buick, safe from the rain, Sabrina felt comfortable with Matt. Her instincts told her he was a good, decent guy and his actions, so far, had proved her right.

"Have you ever been on this road?" Matt drove carefully, which was a good thing since the road began to narrow considerably and still they were climbing. They passed a sign saying DANGEROUS CURVES AHEAD. Sabrina checked her seatbelt. It was loose and seemed to be broken.

"I haven't done much sightseeing since I got here." Sabrina looked out of the car window and saw that the ground dropped away on her side, descending hundreds of metres to the sea below. The only light penetrating the dark night came from the twin beam of the Buick's headlights. Occasionally a bolt of lightning would zig-zag across the sky. She was not one to be nervous, but this road seemed extremely dangerous, especially on a stormy night like this.

"Don't be afraid." Matt sensed her mood completely. "I can drive along this road with my eyes closed."

"I wish you wouldn't." She was able to let out a small laugh, although it didn't completely cover her concern. *I won't look down. Maybe that will solve the problem.*

"I just meant that I've been out here a million times. And I don't mean with girls, although the spot is known as Lovers' Leap." Matt had answered her next question already.

"Lovers' Leap?" Sabrina repeated. "Has anyone ever—"

"Leapt?" Matt finished her question. "No. In fact many changed their minds looking at the view. It makes living in this dull place worthwhile."

"You don't like Innisfree?" Since Sabrina had decided not to look out of the window any more, she turned to study Matt. His profile was illuminated by the instrument panel lights. *How could anyone be so handsome?*

"I've never lived anywhere else," Matt explained. "We Pierces kind of get stuck in one place. My great-great-grandfather moved here and became a logger, then my great-grandfather logged, my granddad worked in the saw mill and now my dad is foreman there. Naturally—"

"They expect you to work in the mill," Sabrina finished for him.

Matt nodded. "Exactamundo. However, they're in for a big surprise. This is one guy who's breaking out."

"Good for you!" Sabrina cheered.

Matt shifted the car into low gear as they climbed further up the windy road. "So how did you end up in Innisfree?"

"It was a bit out of my control." Sabrina slid a little closer to Matt, partly because the drop on her side of the car unnerved her but mostly because she wanted to get closer. "My mother died while we were in Sri Lanka. It was a long drawn-out illness."

Sabrina said this matter-of-factly, covering up the fact that she still missed her mother terribly.

"That explains it," Matt murmured. He squeezed her hand and then put both his hands back on the steering wheel. The car had reached the summit of the rugged mountain.

"Explains what?" Sabrina asked.

"No matter what you do – when you smile or laugh, anything, there's always a look of sadness behind your eyes."

Sabrina clasped her hands in her lap. "I've had some trouble getting over her death. I guess you could say I'm part of the reason – the main reason, actually, that my father returned to the States. I was having a little difficulty with depression. He thought I needed a change."

"But why Innisfree?"

"On my parents' honeymoon, they took a trip up the California coast. They'd met in San Francisco, when they were both students. He was from Boston and she was from Los Angeles. He was sort of a stuffy scholar-type and she was more of a free spirit."

"Sort of like you?" Matt asked.

"Oh, I'd love to think I'm like her, but she was truly an artist. She painted seascapes, mostly, and gardened. She loved exotic flowers. But her favourite flower was the rose. It's funny but wherever she went, the room would smell of roses. Besides painting and gardening, she also loved poetry. Her favourite poem was by William Butler Yeats, called 'The Lake Isle of—"

"Innisfree, " Matt finished for her.

"Oh, do you know it?" Sabrina asked.

"No, but our town was named after that place in Ireland."

Sabrina nodded. "It's a beautifully simple poem. And because 'The Lake Isle of Innisfree' was her favourite poem, my father took her to Innisfree, California, on their honeymoon. My mother loved it here – the gingerbread houses, the mountains covered with redwoods that run right into the sea, the mysterious fog that rolls in without warning. She said to Dad that someday she hoped they could live here. So, when Dad decided I needed to come back to the United States, he chose Innisfree. For her. I thought it was a perfect place for him, too, because he's in the middle of a book. It's about Mother."

The headlights from Oz's old Buick played across a truck parked up ahead on the cliffs. Matt was driving slowly so there was time for Sabrina to look at the parked vehicle as they passed. A couple were inside, making out.

The glare of the headlights made the couple turn briefly and squint right into the light. It was hard to see clearly and Sabrina turned her head, not wanting to embarrass the couple by staring.

Matt slowly drove the car towards the highest part of the cliff. The road ended a tiny way from the edge, and nothing was in front of them except the sky. They were perched on the edge of a towering bluff, hundreds of metres above the dark ocean below. The rain had stopped completely now. The dark, swirling clouds broke and suddenly the night sky was dappled with millions of stars.

"This is it." Matt turned off the ignition and the headlights. They sat there for a moment, the only sound coming from the wind and the surf crashing against the rocks far below. "So...what do you think?"

"Well, it certainly is dramatic. I mean, it's like the end of the earth or something." Sabrina wasn't too comfortable there since they were parked perilously close to the edge.

"I thought you especially would like this spot, since it seems to me that this is about as close as a person can get to God round here. I mean, I know you're into spiritual things." Their eyes were beginning to grow accustomed to the darkness and she could see that Matt was looking at her.

"How d'you know that?" Sabrina asked.

"You said the first day of school that you were 'feeling the vibrations'." Matt leant back against his car door, his elbow resting on the steering wheel, and studied her face. "What are you feeling now?"

"Truthfully?" Sabrina pointed to the cliff in front of them. "I'm a little nervous about where we're parked and..." She took a deep breath. "—what we're going to do, now that we're parked."

"We don't have to do anything," Matt replied, with a shrug. "Except enjoy the view and each other." He chuckled and looked out at the stars. "My little brother, Danny, brought a piece of paper home from school and at the top was written, All About Me. Then underneath were different categories, like My Favourite Colour, My Favourite Food, Things I Like To Do, Things I Want To Do. That's a good way to get to know all about each other. Want to try it?"

Sabrina laughed. "OK. I'll start. My favourite colour is red, although I've been wearing a lot of black lately."

"My favourite colour is blue," Matt replied.

"Naturally," Sabrina said. "It matches your eyes."

"Under the food heading, pizza tops the list, followed closely by root beer and almond fudge ice cream," Matt said.

"What a nutritious meal," Sabrina said,

rolling her eyes. "I love pizza, too—"

"You'll have to," Matt cut in, "if we're going to make this a lasting relationship."

"But I also like curry and other spicy dishes, which—" she pointed one finger at Matt "—you'll have to learn to like if you want to stick with me."

Matt's eyes twinkled. "I like horse riding. OK with you?"

Sabrina giggled. "I love horses, dogs, any kind of animal. I like hiking outdoors but I also love curling up with a blanket, a bowl of freshly popped corn, and watching—

"An old movie," he finished. "Me too." Matt slipped his arm across the seat, behind her, so that his hand was touching Sabrina's shoulder. "OK, we've covered the surface stuff," he declared. "Time to dig deeper."

Sabrina cocked her head. "All right. Here goes. I know I'm in California, and everyone laughs about horoscopes here, always asking 'What's your sign?' but...I *do* believe that the stars seem to be lighting and guiding our way."

"You're talking about astrology?" Matt asked. When Sabrina nodded he said, "You're a Scorpio, right?"

Sabrina's eyes widened. "How did you know that?"

Matt chuckled, slightly embarrassed. "I wish I could say I guessed it, but I happened to be in the principal's office and saw your admission papers on the desk. I took a peek at your birthday."

"So I guess my question should be, what's your sign?" Sabrina said, smiling.

"I'm a Taurus," he confessed. "I looked it up and we're complete opposites. Yet we attract."

Sabrina knew it was true. She could physically feel this attraction. With every moment she was being drawn closer and closer to Matt and she wasn't purposely moving her body in his direction. He was like a magnet.

"I believe," Sabrina continued, "that there is a force beyond our control that guides us to where we must end up being."

"Like you being here with me?" Matt murmured. He studied her face as if he was trying to memorize it. His fingertips brushed her hair and touched her cheek.

"I feel," she said, closing her eyes at the thrill of his touch, " – and don't ask me why, because I don't know – but I do feel you and I have been pulled together by fate. I felt it from the first day

I entered the school."

"I felt it, too," Matt whispered, as their bodies moved closer and closer together. "From the moment I met you, I've just wanted to be with you."

Matt moved his face closer to hers and the world outside the car melted away, dissolved into insignificance. Sabrina was no longer aware of the cliff below, of the dark of the night, of the stars twinkling overhead or any sounds of the outside world. The universe had been reduced to just the two of them, face to face, heart to heart.

Sabrina could smell his spicy aftershave and feel the warmth of his breath on her face. She looked into his eyes, anxiously ready for their first kiss.

Matt's arm wrapped round her shoulder and as their lips touched...

Thud!

Something jolted the car.

Sabrina quickly looked behind her. Their car had been hit, rammed from behind. Now they were rolling forward, sliding towards the edge of the cliff!

"Oh, my god!" Sabrina screamed as Matt struggled with the brake.

But it was too late. They were falling...falling...plunging down towards the dark sea below. The car was scraped and beaten against the rocks as they turned over and over in space.

"Sabrina...no!" Matt screamed.

Sabrina looked into his eyes and watched the panic give way to resignation.

Then there was nothing. Nothing but empty darkness.

CHAPTER FIVE

Sympathetic Venus is making a square to transiting Saturn, which jars your senses. Saturn wants some order and discipline, but with Neptune in Pisces, and Venus in watery Cancer, you are apt to be overtly sensitive. Buy extra tissues. You'll need them.

As the time for the funeral approached, almost everyone in Innisfree put aside what they were doing and made their way towards the hillside cemetery next to the community church. School was dismissed, cafés and shops closed their doors, and sawmills stopped humming. This was a small town, where neighbours stood by each other in times of triumph or tragedy.

Time...

Twelve days had passed since Osgood's car plunged off the cliff. Most people, including the police, had concluded that, since the car was old, the brakes had failed, and Matt had been unable to stop it in time to prevent the horrible accident. No one had any reason to think otherwise.

That rainy night, Sabrina's father had stayed up working on his novel, engrossed in his tale of romance and memories of his dearly-missed wife. Finishing a chapter, he'd come out of his study and glanced at the clock on the living room mantel. It was later than he thought.

He'd wondered why his daughter had not returned before midnight, as she had promised. At one in the morning, Mr Stallings drove to the high school gymnasium but arrived to find the building silent, dark, locked up for the night.

By three o'clock, Mr Stallings had had enough of pacing the floor. He called the police. Naturally, they asked a lot of questions, but Mr Stallings had no answers. By this time, Matt's parents had also telephoned for help.

Although the night officer on duty was sympathetic and promised to interview a few of the kids from the dance the next morning, he couldn't justify waking up an entire town in the middle of the night to try and find a missing teenage couple.

"Kids do crazy things. Maybe they decided to drive all the way to San Francisco. Just for fun. Some time tomorrow you'll get a collect call from Fisherman's Wharf, you'll see."

Then Matt's parents told the police that his car was in the garage. Everyone in Innisfree, including the police, knew that Matt was a good kid. He played football, worked summers as a lifeguard at the community pool, occasionally helped out at the sawmill, and was always round when someone needed a helping hand. He'd never caused anybody any trouble – ever.

Because Osgood was Matt's best friend, the police finally called the Hortons. Oz was still drunk when his parents dragged him to the phone at 5 a.m. No, he didn't know where Matt was. Or for that matter, where his Buick was. A quick check found that it was gone.

The two policemen on nightshift spent the last remaining hours before daybreak searching the streets for a sign of Osgood's beat-up Buick, but with no luck. Matt and Sabrina had vanished.

It wasn't until dawn that a fishing boat spotted a wrecked car on the beach south of town and radioed the police for help. Police cars and ambulances rushed to Lovers' Leap, but it was too late. Osgood's car was so completely demolished, with parts of it scattered across the sand and in the ocean, that it was hard for the police to piece together what really happened the night before.

Tragically Matt had plunged with the car all the way down and didn't survive the impact as the Buick slammed into the rocky surf. It took most of the day to get a crane and lift what was left of the car out of the ocean, then prise Matt's limp body free from the twisted metal.

Sabrina must have been thrown free as the car fell. She'd been found on a wide ledge halfway up the cliff. It was a miracle that she'd landed there with no broken bones, but the extent of her head injuries was still undetermined.

People from the community rushed to help but there was little they could do. Matt's family began to make funeral arrangements. Sabrina's father camped out at the community hospital and prayed.

Sabrina lay in a coma for forty-eight hours. When she awoke, she couldn't recall what had happened, but she sensed immediately that Matt was gone and she began to cry.

Later, the police questioned her about the events of that fateful evening but Sabrina could remember nothing beyond scattered, unconnected things. Leaving the dance with Matt. Driving up a mountain in the rain. The haunting last look on his face as they tumbled into the blackness.

Twelve days later, and still no one had any definite answers. The sunny autumn day and the crisp carpet of red and gold leaves that lay over the ground, stood in contrast to the sea of mourners in sombre clothes flowing through the iron gates of the cemetery.

Sabrina stood at the graveside, her head in bandages, still suffering from the effects of concussion. Although her doctor wanted her to remain in hospital, Sabrina felt she had to be with Matt's friends and family as they said goodbye.

The minister began the service. "We are gathered here today to remember one of our own, Matthew Pierce..."

He had been one of the most popular boys at school, so most of the student body was at the graveside.

Sabrina stood apart from the other kids, wearing the same black dress she'd worn at her mother's funeral. Still feeling weak, she leant on her father's arm for support. Sabrina had been badly bruised by the fall, which made walking difficult. The emotional pain was far worse.

She studied the man and woman standing in front of the polished coffin. Matt's parents were ghostly white, as if all the life had been drained out of their tired bodies. His father, a thick-chested man who was obviously uncomfortable in his ill-fitting black suit, stood stoically, his craggy face a mask of submerged pain. Beside him Matt's mother dabbed mechanically at her red-rimmed eyes. Her shoulders slumped as if the earth beneath her feet was pulling her down.

A young boy, maybe seven or eight years old, stood next to Matt's mother, clutching her hand. With his long blond hair, Danny's resemblance to Matt was uncanny. He was sobbing. Sabrina wanted to wrap her arms round the little boy and weep with him.

As the eulogies continued, first from the football coach and then from the student council president, Sabrina began to feel an overpowering sensation in her body. Something, or someone, was nearby.

Sabrina flinched and quickly glanced over both shoulders. She saw nothing except the mourners gathered to pay their respects.

Maybe it's the painkillers. Sometimes they would shoot little electrical impulses through her body like that. *No, it's something else. There's a strong presence nearby, I'm sure.*

Then the delicious scent of roses filled the air. *Mother!* Sabrina turned, expecting to see her mother standing next to her father, her hand looped lightly through the crook of his arm. But of course, she wasn't there.

Jeff Winstead was the first of a group of students who made their way over to Sabrina to express their concern. He kicked at the ground with the toe of his shoe and murmured, "I'm really sorry about everything, you know?"

Sabrina squeezed Jeff's hand, but there was simply nothing else for her to say except "Thanks."

Osgood wasn't handling Matt's death well at all. He was crying so hard he could barely talk as he gave Sabrina a hug.

Her father told her that Osgood was blaming himself for Matt's death. Others had assured him that it was Matt's idea to take the car to Lovers' Leap. But that didn't seem to help.

"The brakes were just fixed," he sobbed. "I swear."

"Brakes?" Sabrina repeated Osgood's words. Her mind was struggling to make sense out of what was simply senseless.

Jodi Biggs followed Osgood. Her face was flushed red and Sabrina could smell the faint odour of alcohol as she mumbled, "It's so tragic, isn't it?"

It was strange. All of them were treating Sabrina like the grieving widow.

Finally, Blair appeared and wrapped her arms round Sabrina. "I'm surprised to see you here, since you had such a horrible fall. I think Matt would have understood if you hadn't been able to come."

As the friends moved away and members of the school choir began to sing "Amazing Grace", tears streamed uncontrollably down Sabrina's face. She was weeping not only for the loss of Matt but for what might have been.

Her father pulled Sabrina closer to his side, but it was no use. There was no consoling her. The pain ran deep down into her soul.

Sabrina, unable to look at the casket, spun to face the opposite direction. The crowd of mourners were spread out like a blanket of grey and black across the landscape, except for...except for...

Sabrina gasped. *I really must be seeing things!* Someone on the far side of the cemetery was waving at her!

Sabrina blinked her eyes several times and the person's face came into focus. It was Matt! His ghostly image grinned at her mischievously.

Suddenly he was walking towards her, through the crowd.

I've lost my mind! Turning her head frantically from side to side, Sabrina looked to see if anybody else could see what she was seeing. No one paid any attention, even when Matt walked directly in front of them.

Matt had on a blue suit, white shirt and a tie – the same outfit he was wearing when they closed the coffin and brought it from the funeral home.

Sabrina squeezed her eyes shut, certain she was hallucinating. She quickly opened them once more. Matt was still waving and walking in her direction, smiling that unforgettable smile.

Somehow Sabrina found her voice. "Is it really—"

"Me?" he finished for her. "Yes."

Matt winked and Sabrina felt her knees give way. Her father tried to catch her as she slid to the ground. But it was too late. Sabrina had fainted dead away.

CHAPTER SIX

He's somewhere in the room. Even before opening her eyes, Sabrina sensed Matt's presence.

She let her heavy eyelids open slowly. A dozen maroon choir robes hung in a row on a metal rack beside her. A framed print of Jesus surrounded by his disciples was on the wall above her head. Sabrina guessed she was in some sort of anteroom to the church. She knew for sure that she was feeling very uncomfortable.

"She's awake!" Sabrina heard someone say. Having no idea who was with her in this peculiar space, she turned her head in the other direction to have a look.

Ouch! She remembered a moment too late that she was still suffering from concussion and had a large bandage on her head. Quick movements were not a good idea.

Jodi Biggs and Blair Stratton were looking

down at her with a combination of curiosity and concern. Since both girls were wearing black, Sabrina figured that not much time had passed since she had fainted at the funeral.

She did remember feeling as if all the blood had drained out of her face and her knees had simply crumbled beneath her weight.

Jodi looked forlorn and wrung her hands nervously. "Oh, god, I hope she'll be OK."

Blair seemed more in control of her emotions. "Sabrina? Are you awake now? You passed out and your dad has gone to call your doctor."

I don't need a doctor. I've just seen a ghost! Sabrina tried to raise up on one elbow. *Where is he?*

"What a terrible shock!" Blair knelt beside Sabrina

Sabrina's eyes widened. *Could Blair have seen Matt, too?*

"You've been through hell these last few days."

No. Blair was referring to the accident and not Matt's return to his own funeral. Sabrina searched the room for Matt. Unfortunately, her view was blocked by the two girls who seemed determined to play nursemaids.

72

"How are you feeling?" Jodi, who was always hyper, was especially agitated.

"Have any details of that awful night come back to you?" Blair asked.

Sabrina was startled by the bluntness of the question. Undoubtedly rumours were rampant about what Matt and Sabrina might have been doing when they drove out to the cliffs that night. Blair probably wanted some inside information.

I shouldn't be so mistrustful. Maybe they're really trying to help.

"Don't tell them anything!" Sabrina heard a voice say.

Startled, she sat straight up and yelled, "Who said that?"

"Said what?" Blair backed away from Sabrina. She shot a quick look at Jodi, who looked more than ever as if she was about to go to pieces. "I think, Sabrina," she added, "that you'd really better go back to the hospital."

"Up here!"

Sabrina turned in the direction of the voice. It had come from across the room, above a large wooden armoire resting in the corner. Sitting on top, close to the ceiling, was Matt – or, rather, a wavering image of him. "Tell them you're

73

fine."

"I'm not fine!" Sabrina shouted back to the image. To Blair and Jodi it appeared that she was only yelling at thin air.

"That's what I told you – you need to go back to the hospital." Blair was convinced that Sabrina was not a well person.

"Tell them you're thirsty and ask them to get you a drink of water." Matt was feeding her the lines to say, but Sabrina wasn't fully playing along.

"I'm not thirsty." Sabrina yelled this at the corner, in the opposite direction from where Blair and Jodi were standing.

"Nobody said you w-w-were thirsty," Jodi stuttered. She grabbed Blair's arm and hissed, "Who's she talking to?"

"No! I *am* thirsty!" Sabrina screamed her change of mind directly at the girls, then lay back down again. "Please, get me some water."

"Oh, sure, we'll be right back. Come on, Jodi, and show me where the water fountain is." Blair and Jodi tripped over their own feet as they hurried to get out of the anteroom. Both girls were completely spooked by Sabrina's behaviour.

When she heard the door shut, Sabrina raised

her head to look at the chest in the corner again, but Matt was no longer there.

"Over here."

His voice came from behind her. She twisted round to see him sitting in a small chair. Sabrina's eyes began to roll back in her head again.

"Oh, no, you don't!" Matt's voice was strong, although his image was still slightly transparent. "I thought you were made of sterner stuff. You must be – you survived the car accident."

"And you didn't," Sabrina whispered. Although still dizzy, she turned her head to see Matt's reaction.

"No. I didn't."

"I'm seeing things!" She put her hands to her temples. "It must be the concussion." She had heard that people with head injuries often had hallucinations.

"You aren't hallucinating." Matt, as he'd done when he was alive, still seemed to know what she was thinking. "I'm really here. And I think I'm here because of you."

"Me?" None of this made sense to her. It had to be a dream, a very bad dream. She prayed she'd wake up in her own room and find out that Matt, the dance, the drive – none of it had really happened.

"Didn't you say you felt some force had put us together?" He looked at Sabrina, who paused a moment and then nodded her aching head.

"Yes, and I believed that, too."

"Well, I have no idea why I'm here, Sabrina. If you receive any strong feelings about it, please let me know." He leant forward in the chair and ran his hands through his blond hair. "All I know is that I wasn't ready to die."

Sabrina raised her sore body up on one elbow and looked at Matt. She was beginning to wonder if Matt's return might be part of a greater plan – something beyond reason and beyond her control. "I've heard that spirits are sometimes kept earthbound because of unfinished business."

"You mean, like unfinished living?" He looked directly at her, his blue eyes glistening.

"Yes, I guess so." She didn't know what to say. He needed answers that she wasn't able to give.

"Well, it doesn't look like there's any chance of my doing that – living, I mean. Touch me." He reached his hand out towards Sabrina. "Go ahead, touch me."

She hesitated, then slowly moved her hand towards his. Closer and closer, and then...her fingers went right through his arm.

"Oh..." The room spun dizzily, and Sabrina fell back.

Just then Blair and Jodi scurried back into the anteroom carrying paper cups of water.

"Sabrina, take the water and act natural," said Matt, who was still sitting in the chair beside her.

"How are you feeling?" Jodi asked, as she started to sit down in that chair.

"Don't sit there!" Sabrina screamed, causing the already nervous Jodi to jump and spill the water all over the maroon carpet.

"OK, I won't!" Jodi backed away to the far wall and let out a small whimper.

Blair came forward to the cot. "Here, I have another cup of water. Drink it," she said. "And a doctor's outside. He's talking to your dad. I think we'd better clear out of the way."

She was trying to be sweet, but it was clear that Blair wished she'd never tried to help. Jodi's eyes were as big as saucers.

Trying to regain her composure, Sabrina turned her head towards the girls. "Thanks...really."

"No problem," said Blair as she grabbed Jodi's arm and yanked her towards the exit. "Let's go!"

As the two girls reached the exit, Jodi hurriedly whispered to Blair, "I told you she was weird."

Sabrina closed her eyes for a moment. She needed to think, but her head throbbed with a tremendous pain.

There was no way that Matt could be in the room with her. They had just buried him. Except he wasn't in the coffin. He was walking and talking.

Although she'd always professed a belief in spirits and the occult, nothing like this had ever happened before. Her mother had appeared to her when she was asleep, but that was just a dream. Or was it?

Sabrina heard footsteps enter the anteroom and then the sound of her father's comforting voice.

"Sabrina?"

She opened her eyes and smiled at him.

"Oh, good, you've come to." Her father patted her arm. "Honey, I called your doctor at the hospital and told him that you'd fainted. He'd like to see you again, right away. In the meantime, this is Dr Hamill. He was at the funeral and has agreed to take a look at you."

"Hello, Sabrina." A grey-haired, distinguished looking man sat down on the chair beside Sabrina. This time Sabrina didn't yell, since Matt wasn't sitting there any more. The doctor quickly felt her pulse and checked to make sure she didn't have a temperature. "Are you feeling any nausea?"

"No," she replied, wanting to add that she was actually fine. *Except for the fact that I've just seen a ghost.*

"I think your father's right. You need to have your regular doctor check you again. Dizzy spells are not that unusual after such a traumatic event, but why take chances? Why don't you rest here until you feel you can safely walk, and then we'll get you to your car."

"Yes, thanks." She gave him a small smile.

"This is a very sad day for our town. Matt was loved by all of us. I brought him into this world, but never expected to see him go before me." He pursed his lips and rumbled, "We're all going to miss that boy."

Although as a doctor he had probably seen many people die, it was obvious that this particular death had been hard for him. Dr

Hamill rose and walked with Sabrina's father towards the door.

"Sabrina, I'm going to get the car and drive it to the back of the church," her father said. "That way you won't have far to walk. Will you be all right until I get back?"

"Yes, Dad. Thanks...I'm fine now." With that, the two men left the anteroom.

Sabrina raised up on her elbow to look round once more. Matt was sitting next to a window at the far end of the chamber. The sunlight played against his golden hair and, at the same time, the sunrays went directly through him.

"I think I do have some unfinished business." He didn't look at her, but kept looking out the window at the world he'd left behind. "Do you remember the night of the accident?"

"Barely."

"Please think as hard as you can," he urged.

"I remember driving up the mountain road and stopping near the edge of the cliff. I felt afraid."

"Of me?" He moved away from the window and came towards her. "I hope you weren't afraid of me."

"No...just of the cliff, I suppose. I wasn't

afraid of you...then or now." Sabrina meant that, although she still thought it was possible she might be talking to a figment of her imagination.

Maybe it's because I want him to come back so much that I think he's here.

"Do you remember the glare of headlights behind us, when we were sitting in the car?" Matt sat next to Sabrina again.

"Headlights? Now that you mention it, I do remember. Yes, I looked back and saw the lights – yes! Just as we were hit!" This was the first time that she'd recalled that part of the evening.

Matt pursed his lips thoughtfully. "I think, Sabrina, that someone deliberately killed me. And...I don't mean to scare you any more than you already are, but I think they were trying to kill you, too. Since they didn't succeed in getting us both, I'm afraid you might still be in danger."

After a few speechless seconds, Sabrina replied, "But why?"

"Because they probably think you saw them. You weren't supposed to have survived, but since you did you could identify them. No one knows how much you really know."

"I didn't see what kind of car hit us," Sabrina

said, struggling to sit up. "I only saw headlights."

"Yes, but they don't know that and it may come back to you, someday."

"But why would someone want to murder either one of us?" Sabrina asked.

"I don't know." Matt looked into her eyes, with a combination of helplessness and affection. "But I just have a feeling about it."

Sabrina suddenly felt icy cold in the pit of her stomach. She wrapped her arms round herself and shivered. "I think you're right, Matt," she whispered. "Because I feel it, too."

CHAPTER SEVEN

*Scorpio, you have to shake off the blues!
Friends can help you here. Let them in. Sun
moving into jovial Sagittarius this weekend,
will light up the cobwebs in the your mind.*

Sabrina tossed and turned in her bed, trying to find a position that would allow her to sleep. It was useless. Visions of Matt crowded her head, tormenting her, robbing her of much needed rest.

She kicked back the heavy feather comforter and sat up on the edge of the bed. Grabbing the remote control for the television from the bedside table, Sabrina quickly flipped the channels in search of something to take her mind off Matt. Nothing – not the morning talk shows or the silly cartoons or latest music videos seemed to capture her interest. She turned off the television and looked round her world.

The soft grey walls of her room, the nicely framed black-and-white drawings hanging on the wall, all of them done by her mother, the deep maroon carpet – it was cold and unwelcoming to her after two weeks of being in its constant presence. Although she had decorated her world herself only a few short weeks ago, when she and her father had moved into this old house, the space seemed sterile and empty.

Maybe she could read a magazine? Except she'd gone through the stack several times already. She had practically memorized the articles. There was no one she wanted to call on the telephone. She really didn't know anyone in Innisfree, anyway.

Sabrina suddenly longed for Sri Lanka, where her bedroom looked out on a clear blue bay and a pristine white beach, where many pets and art projects filled her time. Solitude in that languid land had meant a peaceful existence.

In the two weeks since the funeral Sabrina had done very little except stay within these four walls, going downstairs only once or twice to have dinner with her father.

Her own doctor had been concerned about

her fainting spell, but further tests had shown that there was little neurological damage. He encouraged Sabrina to return to school whenever she felt like it. But she was too depressed even to dress herself. *How many days have I been wearing the same T-shirt and pair of shorts?* She couldn't remember. Nor did she care.

Matt had appeared to her so clearly at the funeral, but since then there had been no contact. She lay back on the bed again and closed her eyes, trying to feel his presence. *Nothing. Could I really have imagined everything?*

"Sabrina? Are you awake?"

Her father's voice came from outside the door. She quickly pulled the bedclothes over her again, certain he was going to ask her if she felt like going to school today. He asked her this every morning.

"Come in, Dad."

Her father opened the bedroom door and entered with a breakfast tray. Cereal with strawberries, orange juice, a bran muffin – he knew her favourite things.

"How about some breakfast?" he asked cheerfully as he put the tray down on the bedcover. "And why don't I open these curtains and let some sunshine in?"

"I wish you wouldn't." She wasn't hungry, but realized she'd probably lost quite a bit of weight. Maybe she should eat. She broke off a piece of the bran muffin and popped it into her mouth. It tasted like cardboard.

"Sabrina, you can't stay in your room forever." He sat down on the edge of her bed and looked her in the eye. "Why don't you tell me what's troubling you so? I realize that you've been through a terrible time, but you must re-enter the world."

She knew he deserved some sort of explanation, since he'd been so worried and so patient. In the last month he'd constantly attended to her every need and hadn't written a single chapter of his book.

"When your mother died," he said, quietly, "I didn't think I would be able to continue – but I did. With great difficulty, but I did. I brought you here to recover from that. And then another awful thing happens." He put his hands over his face, struggling to control his feelings. "But now you must simply go on because that's what Matt would have wanted you to do."

"I know that, Dad. It's just that I have a very

strong feeling that what happened wasn't an accident."

Her father sighed heavily. "Sabrina, the police made a thorough investigation. Osgood's car was old and in terrible disrepair. They said the brakes must have failed."

"But the feeling is so powerful, Dad." Sabrina curled up next to him. "Mother always said I should trust those feelings."

"And she was right," her father said. "But you need to have something tangible to base them on. And, frankly, you're not going to find out where these feelings are coming from here in your room. Why not go to school?" He sighed heavily. "I hate to see you retreat into yourself like this. Not again."

They both knew what he was referring to. When her mother died, Sabrina had withdrawn completely, barely eating or talking to anyone for months. The hurt on her father's face was almost unbearable. Sabrina hugged him tightly and murmured, "I'm sorry."

Ding-dong!

The doorbell rang downstairs. "Who could that be at this hour of the morning?" Mr Stallings got up to check.

Sabrina followed him out of her room and

watched from the landing.

"Coming!" her father yelled as he reached the hall below. When he opened the door, Sabrina heard a familiar voice.

"Good morning, Mr Stallings. I was wondering how Sabrina's feeling. I'm her friend Osgood."

"Come in, come in. I've heard Sabrina mention you. She's still upstairs in her room."

"No. I'm right here, Dad," Sabrina shouted, hurriedly smoothing her hair in the hall mirror. She glanced at the shadows under her eyes and hoped that she didn't look too awful. "Hi, Oz."

Osgood saw Sabrina and smiled. "Hey, I was just on my way to school and thought I'd check on you. How you doin'?"

"Better, thanks. In fact..." Sabrina paused, trying to muster her courage. "I think I'm going to school today."

"All right! I'll walk you there!" Osgood said.

"I'll hurry and get dressed."

While her father offered Osgood a cup of coffee, Sabrina raced back into her room, threw open her wardrobe door and pulled out a black skirt and sweater. She dressed, then ran a comb through her hair. "Ouch!" It still hurt to touch her head, but she didn't think she looked too awful.

Within ten minutes she and Osgood were out the door and walking down the street towards Innisfree High. She was stunned by how good it felt to be outside in the fresh, clear air. The autumn leaves were falling from the giant elms that formed a canopy over the avenue. After a couple of blocks of walking in silence, all Sabrina could say was, "Thanks for coming to rescue me."

"Rescue? From what?" Osgood used the toe of his hightop sneaker to kick at the leaves covering the walkway.

"From terminal self-pity," Sabrina confessed. "I've been feeling so sorry for myself. But I realize that I only knew Matt for a short time. I mean, you were his best friend and I know you miss him, too."

"More than I can say." Osgood shoved his hands in the pockets of his jeans. "I've known Matt for ever, since we were born, and he was one of the few people who seemed to think I wasn't a major dork." He shrugged. "He was a great guy."

"Yeah." They walked past the gingerbread houses in the old neighbourhood. A few people were out raking leaves and there was the smell of woodsmoke coming from the neighbourhood chimneys. Sabrina kept looking round, half expecting to see Matt smiling at her from behind some tree, but there was no one.

Osgood stopped and took off his glasses. "I still can't believe Matt is gone. I mean, at least twice this week, I went to the phone to call him. I wanted to talk to him about my SAT scores and just life in general and – I know this sounds weird, but I dialled his entire number before I realized he wasn't around any more."

Osgood's voice cracked and Sabrina took his hand. "It's hard. I know. And unfortunately there is nothing you can do but wait for the pain to go away."

Sabrina realized she telling Oz practically the exact words her father had said to her.

Oz took several deep breaths. She could tell he was trying hard not to cry. "I don't mean for this to sound dramatic, but this is the worst time in my entire life. I mean, my best friend in the whole world goes and dies." Osgood slipped his glasses back on his face. "I've been so bummed out about Matt that all I've been able to do is play *Jeopardy*. Last night I won $140,000."

"You did?" Sabrina gasped.

"Well, not really," he admitted. "But if I'd

actually been on the show I would have. I ask you, how can a guy who consistently wins trips to Hawaii and new cars on TV, a guy who can do super-acrostic puzzles in less than four minutes – how can such a genius score so low on the college entrance exams? I mean, I *knew* I'd aced those tests when I took them. I felt it in my bones. I was finished fifteen minutes ahead of everyone else."

It was obvious that Oz wasn't going to let his test scores rest in peace. Sabrina felt sorry for him, which was a nice change of pace since she'd been feeling sorry for herself for such a long time. "I think you must be right," she said. "Somebody screwed up on the grading."

He slipped his glasses back on his face. "But who? And what can I do about it?"

Beep!

Sabrina and Osgood turned to see a yellow convertible zoom up to the kerb next to them. "Sabrina!" Blair Stratton yelled from the driver's seat. "It's great to see you. Look, a bunch of us are going to the Atomic Café after school. Want to come with us?"

Sabrina was poised to say "No", but Osgood jumped in with "She'd love to."

"Excellent! See you later!" Blair threw the

sports car into gear and screeched away, her long black hair blowing in the wind.

"Why'd you accept that invitation for me?" Sabrina gave Oz a small punch on the arm.

"Because you need to get to know people," he said as they began to walk again in the direction of the school.

"Then you're going to have to come with me," Sabrina said, folding her arms across her chest.

"Me? And be with all those snobs? No thanks. I've got a grudge match on *Jeopardy* today. But you go. It's good for you."

They crossed the street and stepped on to the high school campus. As usual, small groups of students were hanging out on the lawn, chatting before their morning classes began.

Sabrina was aware that people had noticed her return to school and were talking about her. She had become a celebrity of sorts in the past month.

"Sabrina!" Jodi came dashing across the lawn. "You're back! I can't talk now, but let's have lunch together."

"I don't get it," Sabrina said to Osgood as they watched Jodi bounce off towards the gym. "Two girls, who barely acknowledged I was alive the first week I was at school, are falling all over themselves now to invite me to do things. Why?"

"It may have something to do with Matt," Osgood replied. "Everyone has been walking round like a zombie. The only thing any of us can do is try and help you because you were his girlfriend."

"But I only knew Matt for a short time." Sabrina murmured.

"Yes, but Matt thought you were special." Osgood smiled at her. "He told me so."

A warm sensation came over Sabrina, followed by the tingly feel of an arm slipping round her waist. She quickly spun round, but no one was there. In the process she dropped all her books and, as she leant down to retrieve them, the school bell rang.

"Need a hand?"

Jeff Winstead, who was nearby, rushed over to help Sabrina and Osgood gather up the notebook paper, which the wind was blowing playfully across the lawn. "How's your head?" he asked, scooping up some pencils which were rolling down the sidewalk.

"Much better, thanks." Sabrina was embarrassed that the entire contents of her notebook were being scattered by the autumn breeze. Her notebook contained a lot of private doodles and some hearts with "Matt and Sabrina" written inside, which she'd drawn before the accident.

"Is your memory coming back?" Jeff asked. "It must be terrible not to remember anything. Of course, I don't remember much most of the time." Jeff laughed. "I'm not like you, Osgood."

"No, you're not," Osgood said, as he picked up the rest of Sabrina's papers. "And that's a relief."

Having gathered most of her things in her arms, Sabrina stood up. She was about to hurry off to class when she felt a sudden bump and all of her school books fell out of her hands again.

"Oh, darn! Now I'm really going to be late for class!" The boys quickly regathered the items, handed them to Sabrina, and they all dashed for the door to the school.

Once inside, Sabrina ran down the hallway to her locker. As she put out her hand to unlock it, the combination whirled by itself and the door opened to reveal Matt standing inside.

"Yikes!" Sabrina squealed.

Matt put one finger to his lips. "Shh!"

"Is it really you?" Sabrina asked, lowering her voice to a hoarse whisper. She had to resist the desire to reach out and touch him, as though he were real.

"Sorry to scare you like that," Matt said, stepping out of the locker. "It's just that I needed to talk to you alone."

"Where have you been?" Sabrina asked, checking over her shoulder to make sure the hallway was empty. "I've been looking and waiting for you for two weeks!"

Matt leant against her locker and smiled. "Does that mean you missed me?"

"Of course I missed you! Terribly!" Sabrina's emotions were churning inside her. She was upset one moment and deliriously happy to see him again the next. "I thought I was losing my mind, that you were just some grief-stricken hallucination. You don't know how awful it's been to have you come back, then lose you again like that."

"Oh, but I do know, Sabrina," he said quietly. "More than you could ever imagine."

The raw pain in his voice brought her up short. "I'm sorry, Matt," she mumbled. "It's just that – well, I know it's selfish of me to say this, but it isn't fair to care for someone so much, and not be able to touch them, or feel them, or be with them—"

"That's not true," Matt interrupted. "You may not always see me, Sabrina, but I'm always with you. Always."

Sabrina took a slow calming breath and then smiled.

"I'm OK now."

"Good."

"You still haven't told me why you vanished for two weeks," she scolded gently.

"I had something important to do," Matt explained. "I went to take a look at Osgood's car – or what was left of it. I had to go to about twenty junkyards all over this part of the state before I found it. Anyway, it was a little difficult to tell, since the car was a dent-mobile to begin with. It's nothing but scrap metal now but I'll swear the rear bumper had a new dent where someone hit us the night of the accident. It was right there in the chrome and rust."

"How can you prove it?"

"I can't prove anything, for obvious reasons," Matt replied, "So it's up to you."

"But who do you think did it?" Sabrina asked, still marveling at how quickly she had become used to his ghostly presence in her life. It felt so right, somehow, as natural as breathing.

"Heather. Or Blair. Both of them are ex-girlfriends of mine."

"But why would they want to kill you?" Sabrina asked dubiously.

"Maybe it was some kind of jealous rage. Look, I know it sounds crazy but I can't think of any other motive."

"That's really stretching things," Sabrina said.

Matt shrugged. "Well, I can't think of any other suspects at the moment." He leant forward. "Listen, why don't you do some investigating? Arrange a meeting with them."

"I'm going to be seeing Blair at the Atomic Café this afternoon. I guess I could ask her a few questions." Sabrina wasn't at all sure that she wanted to find out about his relationship with these other girls. "But how will I know if she's telling the truth?"

"Don't worry," Matt reassured her. "I'll be there with you."

Suddenly Sabrina sensed that they were no longer alone in the hallway. She turned her head slightly and noticed the boy in black, the same one she had seen on the first day of school, and at the gym on the night of the dance, watching her. *I look like I'm talking to myself,* she thought.

The boy seemed about to say something, but then he disappeared round the corner, out of sight.

"Great!" Sabrina threw her arms in the air and turned to Matt. "Now I'm going to get a reputation for being weird."

"I hate to break it to you," Matt said with a chuckle, "but you *are* weird. Weird but wonderful."

CHAPTER EIGHT

The Atomic Café was in the old waterworks, a brick building built over the river at the edge of town. Unused for decades, the structure had been renovated recently into a series of trendy cafés and shops. Water from the river still flowed right through the building, with tables set up on several funky terraces lining both sides of the stream. A series of spidery bridges, held by steel cables, connected the different levels and a huge glass skylight made the entire structure one large atrium. The overall look was spectacular, more suited to San Francisco than Innisfree. From the moment it opened it had become the most popular hangout in town.

Sabrina spotted Blair waving to her from a table on the top level. She began to work her way though the maze-like stairs and bridges, trying to figure out the best way to reach the perch where Blair was standing.

Usually Sabrina liked being near water and

found it soothing, but for some reason, she felt very jumpy this particular afternoon. *Maybe I'm trying to do too much on my first day back out in the world.*

A labyrinth of hallways got Sabrina completely confused and she found she had taken a wrong turn down a dark dead end. Before she could retrace her steps, she heard voices coming from the end of the passage. Peeking round the corner, she saw Jeff Winstead having an intense discussion with Mandy Gibbs, the sophomore from her French class. The girl appeared to be crying and Jeff was angrily shaking his head at her.

"You gotta leave me alone," he shouted.

"But I feel so incredibly guilty," the girl pleaded. "I need to talk to you."

Sabrina was suddenly hit with an image so loud and strong that it nearly knocked her over. Mandy and Jeff, all alone, parked in a truck, caught like deer in a spotlight! Pow! Then the picture was gone. *Was that a memory or a vision?* She took several deep breaths to calm herself.

"Matt, are you there?" she whispered, but there was no answer. *He said he'd be with me and now I don't feel him.*

Without warning, Jeff turned suddenly and caught sight of Sabrina. She ducked round the corner and hurried away, embarrassed at being caught eavesdropping.

After she had worked her way back to the central open area, Sabrina spotted Jodi, staring down at her. Matt was beside Jodi, waving.

"Where were you?" Sabrina yelled at him.

Jodi was completely confused and made a gesture, indicating, "I don't know what you mean."

Matt pointed Sabrina towards the correct suspension bridge linking her to the level where the girls were sitting. Blair, who was drinking a mocha, stood and welcomed Sabrina with open arms.

"How are you feeling?" Blair asked. "All of us have been worried about you." Sabrina couldn't help feeling that Blair was overdoing the concern.

"I'm doing OK, Blair. Not great, but OK." Sabrina ordered an espresso and sat down with the group. "How are you guys holding up?"

"We all really miss Matt," Blair said, leaning over to touch Sabrina's arm. "I mean, there's a giant hole in the school where he used to be."

Jodi nodded, her eyes filling with tears. "And

no one can fill it."

Matt leant forward and whispered, "Now's a good time to ask Blair how she felt about me."

"I can't do that!" Sabrina blurted out. "I just got here!"

Blair and Jodi gave her startled looks and she quickly tried to cover her tracks.

"There I go, thinking out loud again," Sabrina said, blushing. "I thought I should probably get home soon. But I just got here." She shrugged at the girls and giggled, nervously.

"Smooth, real smooth," Matt groaned. Sabrina ignored him and plunged ahead.

"You were really close to Matt, weren't you, Blair?" she asked, shooting a "See? I did it!" look in Matt's direction.

"Matt was practically my best friend." Blair lowered her mauve-shadowed eyelids and sighed.

"Blair is a liar!" muttered Matt. "She barely spoke to me after we broke up."

"After we dated, we talked all the time on the phone," Blair continued. "I used to tell him all about Charles."

"Charles who?" Matt stood up and crossed behind Blair.

"Of course, Matt would confide in me about all of his girls," Blair said, taking a sip of coffee.

"*All* of his girls?" Sabrina raised a questioning eyebrow.

Matt moved back to Sabrina and knelt beside her. She forced herself to look into her coffee cup instead of his eyes. "Believe me, Sabrina, you are the only girl for me."

"I'm glad," Sabrina murmured, taking a sip of the espresso.

"Listen, focus on Blair," Matt continued, speaking directly to her. "Ask her where she was the night of the accident."

Sabrina put down her cup. "You know, Blair, I remember seeing you at the dance the night of the accident, but I don't remember you being with – what did you say his name was?"

"Charles. Charles York." Blair shook her head. "But he wasn't there. Charles came back to Innisfree on the train later that evening, so I left the dance to go and pick him up." Blair folded her arms across her chest. "It looks like your memory is coming back. What else do you remember?"

"I remember the dance and leaving the gym, but not much after that," Sabrina confessed. "I think my memory will come back soon. New images float into my head all the time."

"Uh, oh! Shouldn't have said that," Matt said, leaning back against the iron-cable railing. This level was at least three stories above the river and the railing didn't look very sturdy.

"Am I late?" Heather Deemer asked, hurrying up to their table. "I was looking for Jeff. He's never where he says he's gonna be."

"I just saw him—" Sabrina started the sentence and then froze with her mouth open. *What am I going to say? That I just saw him with Mandy in the hallway, having a fight?* She back-pedalled furiously. "I, um, just saw him in the parking lot. It looked like he was leaving."

Heather seemed really annoyed as she slipped into one of the café's chairs. "You talked to him?"

"No, I just, um..." Sabrina didn't get to finish her fib, since Heather suddenly squealed, "Jeff! Here I am!" He was coming up the stairs.

"Hey, I'm sorry I'm late. I just got here." Jeff nonchalantly pulled up a chair beside Heather and gave her a peck on the cheek. Then he shot Sabrina a threatening look, which clearly meant "Don't you dare say anything about Mandy!"

"Jeff, can I talk to you privately?" Heather grabbed him by the sleeve of his leather jacket and pulled him to the other side of the platform.

Jodi leant in and whispered, "Fasten your seatbelts. World War III is about to start."

"I couldn't believe Jeff at the dance," Blair murmured to the group. "First he screams at Jodi, she runs to the bathroom in tears – and then what does he do? Runs off with the guys!"

"I don't think he was with the guys," Sabrina said without thinking.

Jodi snapped to attention. "Really? Who was he with then?"

Sabrina realized that the girls' gossip antennae were at full alert. "I-I'm not sure," she waffled. "My memory is still kind of fuzzy but I think he was with..."

"Careful!" Matt warned.

Sabrina suddenly gripped the side of her head. "Sorry, it's gone right out of my head. I'm still not thinking straight."

Blair looked disappointed. Then Matt whispered in Sabrina's ear, "I think we'd better talk."

"Now?" she said out loud.

"Yes, now."

Sabrina stood up. If there was any doubt that her behaviour this afternoon had been odd, this cinched it.

"What do you mean – now?" Blair asked after a sideways glance at Jodi.

"I have to go to the bathroom...now," Sabrina said, with a nonchalant wave. "I'll be right back."

She quickly ran down the stairs to the next level, safely away from the girls. Matt appeared in front of her and she followed him past the door to the women's restroom into a long hallway, where they ducked inside a cleaner's cupboard.

"Listen," he started to say, but she interrupted.

"Oh, god, Matt, this is a disaster. Everyone thinks I'm crazy!"

"Crazy is good," Matt reminded her. "It makes them a little bit afraid of you."

Sabrina started to protest but Matt raised one finger. "Listen to what we've discovered. First, it looks like Jeff lied to Heather, and everyone else, about where he was the night of the accident."

"OK," Sabrina admitted, as she tried to find a place to stand comfortably in the dark cupboard crammed with mops and brooms. "I think he was with Mandy Gibbs that night. But I'm not sure where."

Matt nodded. "I'm a little fuzzy on that, too."

Sabrina thought hard, trying to remember more about that evening.

"Blair is acting pretty suspicious, if you ask me," Matt said. "Maybe she's trying to hide her feelings about me."

"Oh, Matt, you heard her. She's crazy about Charles York. So any motive for killing you out of jealousy is shot."

"I think she's bluffing," Matt said, folding his arms stubbornly across his chest.

"Maybe your ego's just a little bruised," Sabrina said gently.

"Ego?" Matt looked genuinely hurt. "I'm just trying to protect you. You call that ego?"

"No, it's just that I don't think pursuing Blair is the way to go. I think you're right about Jeff," Sabrina said, wanting to change the subject. "Did you see that look he gave me when he sat down?"

Matt nodded. "Which is why you have to be careful what you say out there. If it really was Jeff who pushed our car over the cliff, we need to be cagey. He needs to think that you remember nothing."

"OK, sorry," Sabrina said, staring at her feet. "I was just trying to maybe make a few friends."

"First we have to figure out who's the bad guy," Matt reminded her. "Then you can make friends. For now, keep your mind on the investigation."

With that, Matt disappeared.

Sabrina tried to follow him out of the closet, but bumped her nose on the door and knocked over a whole shelf of cleaning supplies. When she finally stumbled into the hallway, she shouted after Matt. "Wait for me!"

"Sabrina?"

She looked up to see two students from school standing in the hall, staring at her.

"Who are you calling to?" one girl asked.

"Um, Blair and Jodi," Sabrina bluffed. "I was having coffee with them and I didn't want them to finish their coffee before me."

The two girls looked at each other and then up at the third level. Sabrina giggled. "They probably didn't hear me. But it was worth a try."

Sabrina hurried back up to the upper level. *They must think I'm a total geek.*

As Sabrina rejoined the group, she noticed Jodi had taken her chair. Matt was standing behind the girls, shimmering slightly. The only seat left was a wooden bench by the railing,

108

near Jeff and Heather. Sabrina picked up her espresso and was just about to sit down when Matt suddenly shouted, "Don't sit there!"

Sabrina lost her balance and fell backwards, bumping into the bench – which seemed to explode! She grabbed at one of the cables holding up the platform and held on for dear life. She watched in horror as splintered pieces of wood from the bench tumbled into the water three stories below.

"Sabrina, are you OK?" Blair cried anxiously. She and the others ran to Sabrina's side.

Sabrina slumped to the floor, clutching the cable with one hand and her now empty coffee cup with the other. "That was a close one," she said in a shaky voice.

"Did you see that?" Heather whispered to Jeff. "She was this close to having a another terrible accident."

"Accident?" Matt pointed to a broken bench leg, the only one which hadn't fallen over the side. The top was sheared off, as if it had been cut. "I don't think so."

CHAPTER NINE

Whether you believe it or not, Scorpio, you're in an up-cycle, with the Sun in fiery Sagittarius, and watery Scorpio making it steam! Your insight is at its deepest, and your intuition tells you the truth, in spite of circumstantial evidence. So your clue for today is – Go for it! Shine that brilliant sunlight on cranky Pluto, and you'll solve your problem.

"*N*eed a ride?" Sabrina heard a deep male voice yell. She had only walked a little way from her house when a huge truck roared up to the curb beside her. It was a black custom pick-up with oversized chrome wheels.

I've seen this truck before, but where?

Her question was answered when Jeff Winstead hopped out of the cab, ran round to open the kerb-side door, and offered his hand to her for support.

Sabrina hesitated, still feeling uneasy from

the day before when the bench had collapsed at the Atomic Café. Jeff and Heather had been the closest to the bench. There had been several lame excuses about how it had happened. Mostly, the building's management was alarmed, and went into overdrive trying to convince Sabrina not to take legal action.

Although they didn't say so openly, Blair, Jodi and the others thought Sabrina was just clumsy because of her lingering head injuries. Ultimately, no one had any answers. Sabrina, however, was convinced someone was out to kill her.

Blair had insisted on driving Sabrina home and she had spent another sleepless night, wondering how many more of these "accidents" she could possibly take.

To make matters worse, Sabrina hadn't seen or heard from Matt since the incident.

"Do you want a ride or not?" Jeff asked, snapping Sabrina out of her daydream.

"Oh...sure. Thanks, Jeff." She took his hand and started to climb up into the high cab when something caught hold of her skirt.

"Are you nuts?" Matt shouted, yanking her backwards. "He's one of our key suspects."

"Let go of me!" she shouted over her

shoulder at Matt.

"Sorry!" Jeff let go and Sabrina fell backwards on to the sidewalk.

"Ouch!" Sabrina winced as she rubbed her ankle. "I think I broke my foot."

"What'd I do? You said to let go!" Jeff sputtered. He spun in a circle with his arms out, to make sure anyone who might be watching could see that he wasn't anywhere near her.

"I'm sorry, Sabrina," Matt said. "I was only trying to help."

"Stay away from me, both of you!" Sabrina struggled to her feet and limped away from the kerb. "I can walk to school by myself."

"That's what I get for trying to be nice!" Jeff muttered. He circled round to the driver's side of his truck and hopped into the cab. Then he shouted through the opposite window, "And I'd keep my mouth shut about the night of the dance, if I were you."

Sabrina's eyes widened. "Then it *was* you with Mandy Gibbs at Lovers' Leap."

A dark cloud covered Jeff's face. "Don't try to say anything to Heather, because she'll never believe you. I let her know you've been hitting on me since you arrived."

"What!" Sabrina gasped.

Jeff put his foot down and the truck zoomed away from the kerb in a cloud of dust.

She dusted off her pleated skirt, looked to see if she'd scuffed the heel of her black loafers, and pulled at her black turtleneck sweater. "What a miserable way to start the day."

Matt appeared again beside her. "I told you that guy was pond scum. Always has been."

Sabrina, still thinking about her foot, glanced sideways at Matt. "And that gives you a reason to make me sprain my ankle?"

"Ever since we were little he's been competing with me. If I earned a badge in Cub Scouts, he'd have to earn two. If I popped a wheelie on my skateboard, he'd have to do it backwards. But it wasn't till we hit high school that he really became impossible. The second Heather and I split, Jeff was on her like glue."

"You think he killed *you* because he wanted *me*?" Sabrina asked, sceptically.

Matt held up his hands. "I don't know. It's possible. He's one strange guy."

Sabrina ran one hand through her hair impatiently. "Oh, Matt! That's silly. Besides, I was in that car. I could have been killed, too. It's a miracle I wasn't."

"Hey, I'm just trying to help solve this

thing," Matt protested.

"If making me sprain my ankle and make a fool of myself in front of everyone at Innisfree High is what you call helping, than I don't need it." Sabrina checked her watch. "Now I'm late for class again. This is so frustrating."

"What?" Matt demanded. "Me? Are you saying I'm frustrating?"

"No. Everything is frustrating. This whole situation." Sabrina flung her arms in the air, accidentally hurling a sheaf of papers across a nearby lawn. "Now look what you made me do."

Sabrina's words clearly stung Matt. He stood with his hands shoved into his pockets, watching her as she ran round the lawn, angrily slamming each page back into her notebook.

"Do you think I want things to be this way?" Matt cried. "Not really existing in any world?"

"Of course not!" Sabrina spun to face him. Tears of frustration burned her eyes. "But I don't know what to do about it."

"Well, it's clear that you don't want me around," Matt said, quietly. Hurt was written all over his face.

"Oh, Matt, I do want you." Sabrina ached to touch him. She reached out her hand and felt nothing. "But as a living, breathing person. Not as a ghost."

"I understand. I'll go away."

Now Sabrina was really crying. She rifled through her shoulder bag for a tissue to wipe her eyes. "Where will you go?" Sabrina raised her head. "Matt?"

She was answered by the faint rustle of leaves on the breeze. Sabrina dropped her bag to the ground. "Matt, wait!"

"Sabrina, are you OK?" a voice asked from behind her.

Sabrina whirled round. "Matt?"

"Sorry." Osgood shrugged in apology. "It's only me." He adjusted his glasses self-consciously. "Is there anything I can do?"

"Yes!" Sabrina picked up her bag and, clutching his arm, cried, "Help me get to school. I'm falling apart."

"Sure."

Sabrina limped along the sidewalk, holding tight to Osgood's arm. "This day has been a disaster from the start."

"Why are you limping?" he asked as they crossed the street.

"Jeff offered me a ride and I started to get into his truck but then I slipped and...it's really too long a story to get into." She dug in her bag once more and, finally finding a Kleenex, blew her nose.

"It's a good thing you didn't get into Jeff's truck," Osgood remarked. "The guy defines the word cretin. He's a jerk to girls, he drives like a madman. In short—"

"He's pond scum," Sabrina finished with Osgood.

Osgood looked momentarily surprised, then nodded. "Matt always despised him." They had reached the other side of the road and the high school was in sight.

"That's what he told me," Sabrina said. "That he and Jeff were rivals." She didn't mention that Matt had only told her that a few minutes before.

"But enough about Jeff," Osgood said, producing a clipboard with a piece of paper covered in signatures. "Will you sign my petition? I'm trying to get the SAT people to retest the entire student body."

"Don't you think it's a lost cause, Oz?" Sabrina said, as they approached the school grounds. "You can't fight the system."

"You certainly can fight it – through the democratic process." Osgood produced a pen from his front pocket. "Now, will you sign it?"

Sabrina stopped to put her books and bag down on a stone bench that sat just outside the schoolyard. "OK. For you, Oz."

As Sabrina was signing her name, Jodi suddenly popped out of the thick hedge growing along the wall. It was an odd place for her to be at this time of the morning – or any time, for that matter.

"Ohmigosh!" Jodi exclaimed. Her face was already slightly flushed but instantly turned a deep crimson. "What are you two doing here? Hasn't school started?"

"Yes," Osgood and Sabrina answered, continuing to stare at her.

"Oh, boy. Oh, boy. Oh...!" Jodi stared back at them, wringing her hands acting as if she'd been caught doing something terrible.

Oz looked at Sabrina and back at Jodi. Then he thrust his clipboard towards her. "Want to sign my petition about the SAT tests?"

Jodi shook her head and backed through the front gates of Innisfree High. "Uh, no, thanks. I really have to get to, um, class."

Then she turned and ran as fast as she could towards the school steps.

Sabrina frowned at Osgood. "What was that

all about?"

Osgood shrugged. "I guess Jodi doesn't like tests."

CHAPTER TEN

Scorpio is always the detective, and is usually tenacious and determined. Use your shrewd Mercury today to think more clearly about events swirling round you.

"You have a new challenge in front of you. I'm not sure what it is, but when transiting Mars beams a laser down on your natal Uranus, it could mean a sudden loss of some kind, or just as important – a sudden blessing. You must look for the good and seek out love. You Scorpios don't always need to be the prickly cactus. Sometimes you must be the aloe vera."

Sabrina knew Madame Zoaunne was trying to be comforting but her words rang hollowly in Sabrina's ears.

"But I have loved," she protested. "And look what happened. Twice my heart has been broken. I never want to love again."

"You have been incredibly hurt." Madame

Zoaunne nodded, her cloudy blue eyes filled with concern. "But use the love that is all round you to help you recover. Heal yourself with love."

Sabrina felt terribly frustrated. She had gone to Madame Zoaunne in search of an explanation for why so many terrible things had happened in her life. But the astrologer didn't have any answers. Only tired homilies that could have come from a fortune cookie. When Sabrina left the tiny trailer she was more depressed then ever.

It was Saturday morning. Her father had gone down to San Francisco for the day. He'd invited her to go along, but she had already arranged her visit to the astrologer. Now she felt anxious. There was no way she'd be able to sit at home.

Sabrina decided to take the bus over to the Centre Mall. Although she didn't quite understand America's love affair with shopping malls, she had been told that this was where most of Innisfree's teenagers shopped, and it was certainly the only place to hang out on a Saturday afternoon.

She'd visited the mall with her father once just after they arrived, to pick up a few odds and ends for school. The building was big, airy and clean, and it did feature a large number of stores for books, clothes and CDs. Still, there was a generic blandness to it all. Sabrina preferred architecture that was a bit more dynamic or unique, maybe because those were characteristics that usually described Scorpios.

"Dynamic," Sabrina chuckled. That was the last word she'd use for herself right now. Her head was still bruised from the accident. The twisted ankle was a little better, although it was bandaged under her red cowboy boots for leg support. But emotionally, she was totally at sea. She had deliberately tried to "get cheery" that morning by dressing in something besides solid black. She had settled on a short black-and-white geometric print pinafore dress over a white T-shirt. She had her large leather bag with her, and a big red scarf tucked inside – for colour. It was a start.

Sabrina got off the bus behind a knot of middle-aged women and followed them across the parking lot to the mall entrance. The minute she stepped into the building a feeling like cool liquid washed over her. She was not alone. Sabrina spun hopefully.

"Matt?"

Could he have changed his mind and come back? No. This feeling was different. This sensation made her feel anxious, uneasy. She tried to shake it off by focusing on window displays. But it didn't help. She wandered from window to window, shooting occasional nervous glances over her shoulder.

Several times Sabrina thought she caught sight of a blond-haired boy reflected in the glass but, when she turned, expecting to see Matt, the boy would be someone totally different – the wrong height, hair colour, everything.

When Sabrina reached the end of the lower level of the mall, she wandered into DrugFair.

Make-up counters were always fun for killing time, whether you were trying on shades of cosmetics you'd never dream of buying or looking for the perfect shampoo scent. Sabrina unscrewed the top of a shampoo marked COCONUT AND MANGOS. It smelled delicious.

"Don't buy that junk, it'll ruin your hair," Blair Stratton said, suddenly appearing next to Sabrina.

"I was just smelling it," Sabrina replied. "Anyway, I read somewhere that all shampoos are pretty much the same. The only difference is the price."

Blair smiled stiffly and swung her own shiny dark hair off her shoulders. "I guess the proof of the pudding is in the eating."

"I guess." Sabrina couldn't believe her social life had been reduced to discussing shampoos.

"Where's Osgood?" Blair asked. "Did you two come to the mall together?"

"Osgood?" Sabrina frowned. "Why would you think that?"

"I heard you were seeing him."

Sabrina blinked in amazement. "Oz walked with me to school on Thursday, if that's what you mean. But I'm not seeing him, and I have no idea what he's doing today. Or any day, for that matter."

Blair shrugged. "I was just curious. He's really a nice guy, though I wish someone would talk him out of that obsession with the SATs."

"I take it you did well on your test," Sabrina replied.

Blair met her gaze evenly. "I did great."

"Then you shouldn't be worried about taking the test again," Sabrina said.

Blair's right eye twitched and then a slow smile spread across her face. "I'm not worried. I just don't want to waste my time." With that Blair turned and marched out of the store.

Sabrina watched her leave. *Hmmm. That was odd.* Blair had appeared out of nowhere, asked about Osgood and then she was gone. Sabrina decided to leave, too, but movement in the next aisle caught her eye.

Jodi Biggs was looking at a display of clocks.

Sabrina was about to say hello when Sabrina noticed Jodi take an electric alarm clock off the shelf, quickly slip it in her bag, and walk briskly out of the store. Shocked by what she had just seen, Sabrina couldn't help but follow Jodi into the mall.

Jodi walked two or three stores away and sat down on a bench under a fake palm tree. Sabrina paused in front of a Banana Republic store, and watched to see what would happen next. Jodi took the alarm clock out of the box it came in, popped the plastic front off of the clock, then broke off the second hand. Next she put the clock back into its original packaging.

Then Jodi pulled a DrugFair shopping bag out of her bag, dropped the clock inside, and walked away from the bench. Sabrina followed, keeping her distance hiding behind pillars.

Jodi returned to the drugstore and stopped an assistant. Sabrina moved behind a tall display of video cassettes so that she could hear what Jodi said to the woman.

"I bought this a few days ago and I think the clock is defective. See?" Jodi held up the alarm clock. "It's missing the second hand. I've lost the receipt, but you can tell from the price tag on the box that it was from your store. So I'd like a refund, please."

Sabrina was amazed to hear Jodi's routine. By her confident attitude, it was pretty clear Jodi had pulled this scam more than once.

"Of course, miss." Without hesitation, the assistant went to the nearest cash register, handed Jodi a handfull of bills and some change.

"Thanks very much," Jodi said pleasantly. She left the store and headed up the escalator to the top floor of the mall. Sabrina continued to follow her, curious to see what would happen next. Then Jodi ducked into a clothing store called The Yellow Brick Road and started browsing through a rack of sweaters on sale.

Sabrina tried to sneak into the store behind her but Jodi spotted her. "Hi, Sabrina, what a surprise! I didn't see you there."

"I, um," Sabrina stammered, "I was looking for a sweater to go with a new pair of jeans I just got."

Jodi cocked her head and looked at Sabrina's outfit. "Does it have to be black? Because these are all bright colours."

Sabrina winced. "Black seems to be my shade. But I'm open to exploring other options."

"Like navy blue?" Jodi joked.

"Who knows?" Sabrina struck a dramatic pose, with her arms outstretched above her head. "Maybe I'll go completely berserk and wear yellow or pink."

Jodi threw her head back and laughed. She seemed nice and much less jumpy than usual. Except for the episode of the shoplifting, Sabrina could imagine herself spending a pleasant afternoon with her. But just to be on the safe side, she decided she'd better ask Jodi a few questions about the night of the accident.

"You know, Jodi, ever since the accident, my mind's been a little blurry about things. Do you mind if I ask you a few questions?"

Jodi, who was now flipping through the leather skirts on one of the circular racks, paused for only a second. "No, go ahead."

"When I left the dance, you had already left before me, right?"

"Um-hum." Jodi didn't look up and

continued to look through the skirts.

"I heard that other people were at Lovers' Leap and—"

Jodi snapped her head round. "I didn't leave the school grounds, if that's what you're asking."

"No," Sabrina back-pedalled. "I wasn't. I just wondered if you knew who was at the cliff that night."

Suddenly Jodi looked over Sabrina's shoulder and gasped, "Uh, oh. I'd better leave."

Sabrina spun to see one of the salesladies making her way towards them.

"That lady has it in for me," Jodi confessed as she hurried towards the exit. "Ever since I returned a pair of slacks she claimed didn't come from this store." Jodi was almost running towards the exit. "I swore I'd never shop in here ever again."

Jodi raced back into the mall, with Sabrina right on her heels. At the exit doors, Jodi turned and leant towards Sabrina, whispering, "Listen, I've gotta get home."

Sabrina couldn't help recoiling. Up close, Jodi reeked of alcohol.

"Bye!" Jodi called as she raced for the big glass doors. "I'll catch you later."

Sabrina cocked her head as an image suddenly formed in her brain. At first it was cloudy, but then it became clear. She could see Jodi standing by the cashbox at the dance. Then she flashed on another image of Jodi taking something from the cashbox and heading out the back door.

Finally, she remembered Jodi stumbling out of the bushes at school. It seemed pretty clear that Jodi was shoplifting to buy booze.

Sabrina glanced at the doors leading outside, and once again saw a boy's reflection in the glass. But this time it was the dark-haired boy in black. He was standing a few metres behind her, staring. She spun, startling him so much that he bolted.

"Wait!" Sabrina called after him. "What is it you want?"

The boy headed into the mall's Food Court, where neon signs flashed above the fast food restaurants, and groups of noisy kids hung out at the tables. The entire area was so crowded that it was hard to keep up with the quick-moving boy.

Sabrina followed as he cut through the queue at the Tasty Burger and headed towards Pizza Express. In her hurry she accidentally knocked a girl's tray of pizza out of her hands. "Excuse me!" she shouted. There wasn't time to stop and apologize. "I can't let this guy get away."

The mystery boy headed towards the entrance to the twin cinemas. Unfortunately for Sabrina, a crowd was coming out of the matineé and he was swallowed up by the mob of moviegoers.

Sabrina stopped and rubbed her eyes. *Maybe he's a ghost like Matt. Or maybe they're both just figments of my imagination.* Sabrina took a shaky breath. *I think I'm losing it.*

Just at that moment a firm hand grabbed Sabrina's arm from behind.

"Blair said you were here." It was Heather Deemer, and she didn't look happy. "I need to talk to you."

Heather's long red nails dug into Sabrina's arm, making her wince with pain. "Fine. But let go of my arm, will you? That hurts."

Releasing Sabrina's arm, Heather hissed, "Stay away from Jeff. I don't know what girls do in Timbuktu, or wherever it is you came from, but out here, when a couple is going steady, other girls butt out."

Sabrina frowned. "What are you talking about?"

Heather put her hands on her hips. "Don't play that amnesia thing with me. I happen to know your memory is fine."

Sabrina was starting to get really irritated with all of the students at Innisfree High. "Look, Heather. You can keep Jeff. I wouldn't want him if he were the last guy on the planet."

Heather smirked. "You didn't feel that way at the dance."

"You're not making any sense," Sabrina said, rubbing her arm where Heather's nails had dug in. "You know I was in the car with Matt when the accident happened."

"You really got round that night," Heather said, narrowing her already beady eyes at Sabrina. "Everyone saw you drag Osgood off the stage and go out the back with him! And not twenty minutes later, I have witnesses who'll swear they saw a dark-haired girl getting into Jeff's truck. That had to be you!"

Sabrina hesitated for a second, wondering if she should mention Mandy Gibbs. *No, let her find out from her so-called friends.* "Look, Heather, this is too ridiculous to even discuss. In the first place, I'm not the person you should be talking to. Talk to Jeff. He's the one hitting on anything with a heartbeat."

"*What*?" Heather shouted indignantly.

"Go yell at him." Sabrina stormed out of the mall and followed the street away from home, her school and the whole terrible town. Too angry and hurt to think, Sabrina let her feet lead her. It was a great shock when she found herself in the one place she had intended never to visit again.

The outline of the small white church loomed starkly against the deep blue sky. Row upon row of marble and stone monuments angled out before her. She was standing just inside the iron gates of the cemetery where Matt was buried.

CHAPTER ELEVEN

Sabrina took great care to avoid going anywhere near Matt's grave. Instead, she climbed a small hill and collapsed beneath a large oak tree. It had scattered a blanket of beautiful red and orange leaves that looked as inviting as a big soft bed, so Sabrina stretched out for a rest. Her ankle ached and she was exhausted from her mad dash through the village of Innisfree.

After she caught her breath, Sabrina sat up and looked out at the rows of marble gravestones and the wide blue river beyond. The serene beauty of the setting stood in contrast to the torment Sabrina was feeling inside.

I wish Matt was here.

"I am," she heard Matt answer.

I'm just dreaming, Sabrina thought, closing her eyes.

"No, I really am here."

Sabrina opened her eyes and Matt was sitting on the hill beside her. "I was hoping against hope that I would see you again," she said. "I wished it."

"Your wish is my command," Matt said with a smile. Then he turned his head to look out at the view. "This isn't such a bad place to be. I've always loved the view from up here. You can see my house over there and, beyond it, the school and the river."

The afternoon sun was on Matt's face and in profile he looked very handsome. Sabrina ached to touch him but knew she couldn't. She pointed towards the west. "And the ocean's over there. It's spectacular, isn't it?"

"Yes," Matt said, wistfully. "I like this place. Maybe I'll come back here someday."

Goose bumps shot up Sabrina's arm. "Come back? How do you mean?"

"Sabrina." Matt faced her. "Do you believe in reincarnation?"

"You mean, like coming back as a cat?" she said with a grin.

"Yes, well, sort of. But I'm talking about the possibility of coming back to this earth and living another life."

"In a different body?" Sabrina asked.

"Yes."

Sabrina thought about Madame Zoaunne's prediction that she would have many eccentric friends in her lives. "I think I do," she replied.

"Good." He nodded his head several times. "Good."

Sabrina cocked her head, squinting one eye shut. "As long as we're asking questions, I've got one for you."

"Fire away."

"Where do you go when I don't see you? I mean, how do you spend your days?"

"Sometimes I just...am. And sometimes I exist and go places." Matt waved his hand over a pile of red and gold leaves. They suddenly leapt in the air, whirling like a tiny leaf tornado, then settled back on the grass. "After I left you at the mall—"

"You did?" Sabrina cut in. "I didn't know you were with me at the mall."

He smiled mysteriously. "I'm your guardian angel, remember?"

Sabrina recalled catching sight of his reflection in the store windows. But whenever she turned, he had disappeared.

"I spent the rest of the day with Osgood," Matt continued. "And I have to say I'm worried about him."

Sabrina nodded. "The test scores are driving him, and everyone who comes in contact with him, crazy. He's obsessed."

"Osgood has always prided himself on being a good student and head of the class," Matt said. "But now he's taken this competition thing too far. This afternoon he watched four episodes of *Jeopardy*, right in a row. The guy tapes them on his video and plays them over and over. Today he won a Jeep Cherokee, a trip to Hawaii and, as Oz said to no one in particular, a lifetime supply of dog chow."

They both laughed at that.

"Then Oz disguised his voice and called the local radio talk show," Matt said. "There's this psychologist who's supposed to help you with your problems. Well, guess what Oz's problem was?"

"His test scores?" Sabrina was so sure of her answer that she laughed when she said it.

"What else? Why disguise his voice? Everybody in town knows about the test. The shrink even knew it was Osgood, you could tell. Then Oz did the weirdest thing I've ever seen anybody do. He blindfolded himself and put together a jigsaw puzzle. In under five minutes."

"You've got to be kidding?" Sabrina cried.

Matt raised one hand. "I swear he did. I think the guy is starting to crack."

Sabrina folded her arms across her chest. "It sounds like he spends too much time alone. Maybe I'll give him a call."

"Would you?" Matt asked. "It would mean a lot to Oz. And to me, too."

"Of course I will."

"Good." Matt looked back over the valley. "I think I'd feel a lot better about leaving, knowing you two were friends."

"Leaving?" Sabrina sat bolt upright. "What do you mean? Now, or for ever?"

Matt looked back at her. "Not at this moment. But I have a strong feeling that my time here is nearly finished."

"But you can't just give up," she protested.

"I wouldn't be giving up. I'd just be moving on."

"Oh, Matt!" Tears clouded Sabrina's eyes and she turned away from him to face the valley. The sun was beginning to slip into the ocean, turning the sky as red and gold as the autumn leaves.

Matt leant towards her. "Listen to me, Sabrina. It won't be for ever. One day you'll be walking down the street, or going up the steps of the library and someone will stop you—"

"You?"

"Maybe not me as I am now, but it will be me."

Sabrina bit her lip, trying hard not to cry. "But how will I know it's you?"

He took a moment to look at her face, as if he were memorizing every feature, and then he whispered, "Don't worry, you'll know."

Sabrina reached into her bag for a tissue. Instead her hand touched something sharp and painful.

"Yeow!" She jerked her hand out of the bag. Blood was dripping from several cuts on her hand.

Matt peered inside her bag. "It's full of razor blades! And there's a message on a piece of paper." He tilted his head to read it. *What's done is done. Leave the past alone.* Matt looked at Sabrina. "Who could have done this?"

"I don't know," Sabrina cried, pulling her long red scarf out of the bag and wrapping it round her hand to try and stop the bleeding.

"Who were you with today?" Matt asked.

Sabrina bit her lip, trying to get past the pain. Her skin stung as if twenty tiny little paper cuts had just had salt poured into them. "Jodi, Blair and Heather. If you were there, you should remember."

Suddenly a shadow loomed behind Sabrina. She felt a presence and screamed, "Who's there?"

"It's just me." The tall, lanky boy was standing a few metres away staring at Sabrina.

"Osgood! What do you think you're doing, sneaking up on me like that?"

Sabrina looked at her cut hand. It was still bleeding profusely and the pain made her irritable.

"I didn't sneak up," he said defensively. "You were talking to yourself and I didn't want to interrupt. What happened to your hand?" Oz didn't come any closer to where Sabrina was sitting.

"What does it look like? I cut it." She looked at Matt, unsure whether she should tell Osgood about the razor blades.

"Do you want me to help? I have to warn you, though, that I faint at the sight of blood." Osgood wasn't kidding and seemed reluctant to get near her.

"Then don't help me." She wound her scarf round her hand again. It seemed to slow the

138

bleeding, but the pain wouldn't ease up. Sabrina let her frustration out by yelling, "For heaven's sake, Osgood, what are you doing here?"

"I might ask you the same question." He looked a little queasy. "A cemetery isn't exactly where I'd expect to find you." Osgood reached into his pocket, pulled out a white handkerchief and offered it to her. She started to take it, then hesitated.

"Don't worry. It's clean. I didn't blow my nose on it." He handed it over and she began fashioning a rather elaborate, artistic bandage out of the scarf and handkerchief. Even at her worst, Sabrina could be creative.

"It's funny," Oz said, shooting a glance towards Matt's grave on the far side of the hill. "But I've had such a strong feeling about Matt all day that I had to come to the cemetery. Then I got this weird note and I felt I had to get out of the house." He reached in his pocket and pulled out a rumpled, yellow card. "See?"

Oz held the card out to Sabrina, but she said, "Read it to me. I've got my hands full."

"Well, there's nothing to read, really. It's somebody's old report card." He swallowed nervously. "But it was tied to a rock that came sailing through my bedroom window."

Matt moved closer to get a look.

"It says on it, in red ink, YOU'LL REGRET THIS!" Osgood shook his head. "Regret what? It's not my report card, since I make all A's and this idiot makes C's. See, the name's been torn off the top, but it's from last semester."

Matt looked at Sabrina and murmured, "This must have happened after I left Oz's house today. Poor guy."

"I can't figure out why anybody would toss their report card at me, unless it has something to do with my petition."

"A lot of kids don't want the retesting to go through," Sabrina replied. "They figure once was bad enough."

"I thought about checking the class schedule to find out whose card this was, but I figured it would be a waste of time."

"Yeah, it seems pretty silly," Sabrina agreed.

"But then the worst thing happened on the way here," Osgood said. "I passed Blair on the street and she was literally dancing for joy."

"Why would she be dancing?" Sabrina asked.

Osgood seemed to physically turn green. "Blair got accepted to Stanford. Can you believe it?" He threw his arms in the air. "The

140

girl in school most likely to flunk a test got accepted to one of the toughest colleges in the country."

"Really?" Sabrina frowned. "Maybe her father bought her a place in the school. I hear they're pretty rich."

Osgood shook his head vigorously. "You can't buy off Stanford. Everyone is rich there."

Sabrina turned to Matt. "I wonder if Jodi is going. Those two go everywhere together."

"Not any more," Osgood replied. "I was at the grocery store yesterday and saw Blair and Jodi having an argument in the parking lot. Jodi asked Blair for money, and Blair refused to give her any. Jodi was furious, and shouted, 'I can't believe it. After all I've done for you."

"I wonder what that meant," Sabrina said, touching Osgood's arm.

Osgood shrugged. "I'm not sure, but your name came up and so did mine."

"How about mine?" Matt asked.

"No, I don't think so," Osgood replied. "I couldn't hear everything they were saying, but it had something to do with—" All of a sudden Osgood realized who he was talking to, and screamed.

Sabrina pulled back her hand in alarm.

"What's the matter, Oz?"

"I swear, I'm losing my mind!" Osgood cried. "I...I...was just talking to...to *Matt*!" He was pale and shaking.

Sabrina was equally confused, and looked at Matt. "What happened?"

"Who are you talking to?" Osgood stepped away fearfully, his eyes darting from side to side.

"I have no idea." Matt moved closer to Sabrina. "You were touching Osgood when he saw me, right? Maybe you should touch him now, and see if it happens again."

"All right." Sabrina walked towards Osgood. "Now hold still, Oz. I'm going to touch your arm."

"Stay away from me!" Oz backed up until he bumped into a large, cold gravestone. "Aaah!" he screamed again.

"Be quiet. Just let me touch you." Sabrina put her hand on Osgood's arm once more, and waited to see if he could see Matt. "Do you see anything?"

Osgood's mouth dropped open in disbelief. His mouth worked soundlessly for a moment until finally he croaked, "It's...it's Matt."

"Can you really see me, old buddy?" Matt

smiled at his friend.

"Yes, I can. See you, hear you – what's wrong with me?" He was practically in tears. Sabrina kept a firm grip on his arm.

"Nothing, Oz, nothing at all," Matt said, beaming with delight.

Sabrina was thrilled that Oz could actually see what she'd been seeing for weeks.

Osgood, however, was a mass of Jell-O. "This is too weird, even for me!" he moaned, collapsing to his knees. "It goes beyond the realm of possibility and into the world of ectoplasm and *Ghostbusters*."

Matt, not wanting to scare his friend, kept his distance but spoke in a soothing voice. "I like to think of myself as more of a spirited observer."

Osgood looked up at Sabrina who shrugged. "I know. It's hard for me to accept, too. But that *is* Matt. And you and I are standing here looking at him and talking to him."

Osgood spun to face Matt. "OK, if it's really you, what's my mother's maiden name?"

Matt frowned. "How should I know?"

"Why'd you ask him that?" Sabrina asked.

"Because at the bank, that's the one question they ask when you are opening an account. That's how they identify that it's really you."

"I don't know your mom's maiden name," Matt said, "but I do know that in the back of your closet is a shoebox labelled 'Important Papers' that you have never shown to anyone but me."

"What's inside it?" Osgood demanded.

"Trotsky," Matt said simply.

"Who or what is Trotsky?" Sabrina asked.

"Osgood's first big experiment. When his hamster died, he'd been reading a lot about Egypt and he decided to try to mummify his pet. He never told a soul about it except me." Matt turned to Sabrina. "Now you are the only other living person who knows about Trotsky."

Osgood's baffled expression turned to one of glee, as he slowly rose to his feet. "Do you realize – if all this is true – what this means? Matt, you could be my science project. I could win the State Science Fair! Win a scholarship!" Osgood pumped his fist in the air with excitement. "This is way too cool!"

"Calm down, Osgood," Matt said. "I can't be your science project. It's not any sort of joke that I'm here now."

"So who's joking? We could go on TV, become famous, win the Nobel Prize." Osgood was so excited that he jerked his arm away from

Sabrina. Immediately he couldn't see Matt any longer. "Where'd he go?"

"I'm afraid you have to hold on to me, Oz," said Sabrina. "And I'm not about to be part of a display at the science fair. I'd have to touch everybody that strolled by in order for them to see Matt. It sounds more like a sideshow act at the circus."

"We could do that! Let's join the circus!"

Sabrina couldn't help laughing.

"We could call ourselves The Amazing Oz and his beautiful assistant, The Exotic Sabrina!"

"I like The Amazing Sabrina better," she corrected. "After all, I'm the one with the power to see Matt. You wouldn't have an act without me!"

"Would you two get real?" Matt scolded. "I'm not here to be in any freak show. We're trying to find out who killed me."

"We are?" Osgood suddenly stopped laughing. "I thought the brakes on my car failed."

Sabrina felt embarrassed at how silly she and Osgood were behaving. "I'm sorry, Matt, I guess Oz and I got carried away."

"Forgiven," Matt said, with a warm smile.

Osgood, who had finally calmed down,

stared at Matt for a long time. Then he said in a hushed voice, "It *is* you. It's really you."

"It's really me."

"Does this mean you're not really dead?"

Matt shook his head. "That can't be changed."

"But how...? Why...?"

"It's complicated," Matt said, shrugging. "I don't understand it myself. I just know that somehow it's connected to Sabrina. She's some sort of channel."

"Oh." Oz nodded. "I've read about that." He scratched his head. "Wait a minute, wait a minute. You said something back there about someone killing you?"

"Right." Sabrina nodded.

"Listen, Oz," Matt said, seriously. "The car didn't just roll over the cliff. We were pushed." Matt sat down under a tree. Then Osgood and Sabrina, still holding on to his arm, sat down too.

"We've been trying to reconstruct the events of that evening," Sabrina explained.

"I can't remember anything," Matt went on, "and Sabrina only has some vague, unconnected images of what might have happened that night."

"Well, since I was kind of out of my head," Oz said sheepishly, "I don't think I can be much help."

"Do you think the razor blades in my bag and that rock thrown through Oz's window could be connected?" Sabrina asked Matt.

"What razor blades?" Oz asked.

"Someone put them in my bag when I was at the mall. That's how I cut my hand." She held up her homemade bandage.

"Don't let go," Osgood cried. "I can't see Matt if you let go." Sabrina quickly put her hand back on Osgood's arm.

"It was a warning to leave the past alone," Sabrina continued. "To just forget everything."

"Why don't we start at the beginning and review the events the night of the dance," Matt said, trying to keep them on track. "And see what we come up with."

"OK." Sabrina got up on her knees without letting go of Osgood. "I think I saw Jodi steal money out of the cash-box. Did you?"

"No, but remember I wasn't seeing so well." Oz paused, then said, "I did, however, hear some of the other cheerleaders mention later in the week that they didn't make any money out of the dance. They thought that was odd, since so many people bought tickets."

"Did you see or hear anything about Jeff going out with Mandy Gibbs that same night?" Sabrina asked.

"He went out with Mandy?" Osgood was amazed. "But what about Heather?"

"They had a fight at the dance," Matt explained. "It was pretty intense."

Osgood winced. "Guessed I missed that, too."

"Just tell us what you do remember," Sabrina urged.

Osgood scratched his head. "Well, after I issued my Osgood Challenge, you guys drove me home, where I passed out from too much spiked punch." He made a sour face. "That was Jodi's doing."

"You know that Jodi has a drinking problem?" Sabrina was surprised.

Osgood nodded. "She hides bottles all over the place. I found about twenty behind that bush she came out from the other morning!" He wrinkled his nose. "Peppermint schnapps and peach brandy."

Suddenly Sabrina heard movement in the leaves behind the tree. She quickly wheeled round and saw the boy in black. He saw her and

148

stumbled backwards, ready to run away.

"That's it!" she declared, hopping up and letting go of Osgood. He and Matt had no idea what Sabrina was yelling about. "It's time to confront that kid once and for all!"

CHAPTER TWELVE

"*C*atch him!"

The boy ran incredibly fast and Sabrina was hindered in the chase by her bad ankle and the fact that she was wearing cowboy boots. But Osgood, with his long legs, was able to keep up with him.

They branched out, hoping to trap the boy against the tall iron fence separating the church from the graveyard.

Just as the mystery boy reached the fence and scrambled to climb over it, a breath of wind seemed to catch him and throw him to the ground.

Naturally, the boy had no idea what caused him to fly off the fence, though Osgood and Sabrina did. They leapt on him and pinned him face down.

"Who are you and what do you want?" Sabrina twisted the boy's arm behind his back with her good hand while Oz sat on the kid's legs. The boy looked afraid, although he was wiggling and kicking, trying to get free.

"Just settle down! We're not going to hurt you!" Osgood said. At the same time the boy got one of his legs free and did a backwards donkey kick that sent Oz's glasses flying. "Hey! Where'd they go?"

"I know him," Matt told Sabrina. "His name is Will Stegeman and he used to live on my block. Let him go."

"If he's so nice, why has he been following me?" Sabrina asked.

"Let him go!" Matt's voice was firm.

Neither Osgood nor the boy could hear Matt's side of the conversation, although Oz now had the advantage of at least knowing Sabrina wasn't talking to herself.

Before she could respond to Matt again, the boy began to scream and cry, "I did it! I did it! I killed Matt!"

"What?" Sabrina was puzzled.

"I killed him!"

"You did? How?" Osgood asked.

Sabrina let the kid sit up. Tears were streaming down his face as he confessed to Osgood, "I was the person who fixed your brakes two days before the accident."

Osgood was stunned. "You work at Stegeman's garage?"

"Stegeman's my dad. He's teaching me to be a mechanic. He let me fix your brakes, and then they failed and Matt went over the cliff."

He was almost hysterical now. Sabrina put her arm round the boy's shoulder. "It wasn't you, Will. Our car was hit from behind. The gears popped into neutral and we went over the edge."

"Are you sure?"

"Positive."

"I never paid the bill for that brake job," Osgood said as he brushed leaves off his shirt. "Do I have to pay it now that the car is wrecked?"

"I don't know." Will continued to weep.

"I've seen you at school," Sabrina said. "You must be a couple of years younger than us, right?"

Will nodded. "I'm a freshman. Are you sure I didn't cause the accident?"

"Very sure." She smiled, trying to reassure the boy.

"I've been so worried. Matt was really nice to me. Although he was a big-shot jock, he always took time to talk to me. He wasn't a

152

snob. See, a lot of kids make fun of me cause I'm small for my age. Anyway, Matt didn't care about that." He started to cry again. "I miss him a lot."

"Touch his arm for just a second, will you, Sabrina?" Matt said, moving directly in front of the boy. Sabrina reached over and touched Will's arm.

"Will," Matt murmured. "I will always be your friend."

The boy blinked his eyes. He seemed to see Matt for a moment and be reassured. Then Sabrina let go and Matt was gone.

Osgood adjusted his glasses. "I remember you. You used to live near Matt's house. Where'd you go?"

"My family moved across town," Will said. "We live next door to Dr York."

"As in Charles York?" Sabrina asked, shooting a sideways glance at Matt. "Blair Stratton's boyfriend?"

"Charles is my neighbour but no way is he with Blair. She's a major pain, always calling him and driving by his house, but he's already got a girlfriend at Stanford. I met her when she came to meet his parents. I think that was the weekend of the dance."

"Did you hear that, Oz?" Sabrina cried. "That means Blair didn't go to the train station to pick up Charles the night of the dance."

"Right," said Osgood, sharing Sabrina's excitement. "So where did she go?"

"I don't know where she went," Will replied. "But I do know that she left the dance in a green Volvo station wagon, which was weird since Blair drives that little yellow car."

There was a pause as Sabrina looked at him and Oz.

"A green Volvo? Are you sure, Will?"

"Yeah. I was in the parking lot 'cause I wanted to talk to Matt," Will explained. "But I didn't get the chance because you were with him. Anyway, just after you two drove away, I saw Blair get into that Volvo. The paint was peeling off and I remembered thinking that someone had done a really sloppy paint job."

"Maybe the Volvo is the Stratton's other car," Matt said to Sabrina.

"I think we should go over to her house and take a look," Sabrina replied. "Like right now." She got up off the ground, dusted herself off, collected her bag and checked her bandage. The three boys followed her out of the cemetery.

"There's just one problem," Sabrina said,

when they were standing on the sidewalk. "I haven't any idea where Blair lives."

"Come on, I'll take you there!" Osgood ran for his bike, which was resting against the cemetery gate. Will's mountain bike was nearby. Sabrina looked back to see if Matt was with them. He winked and waved — then vanished.

Sabrina hopped on the back of Osgood's ancient Schwinn and held on for dear life as they set off down the hill.

Night was falling as Osgood guided them back through town into a new development close to where the river fed into the ocean. The sign at the entrance said RIVERBEND.

Sabrina had never been there before and was amazed to see the expensive, contemporary, glass and wood homes that jutted out over the coastline. Blair's house was the largest one in the neighbourhood. Sabrina was disappointed to see a Lincoln Town Car and the little yellow car parked in the driveway.

"No sign of a Volvo," Osgood said with a sigh. "I guess we were wrong about Blair."

"Wait a minute," Will rasped. "Look over there, by the hedge."

Sabrina and Osgood peered in the direction

Will was pointing. Barely visible behind a thick green hedge was a dark green Volvo station wagon.

"That's the car!" Will whispered. "See the crummy paint job?"

Sabrina headed for a group of low evergreens and ducked down behind them. Oz and Will followed with their bikes, but Osgood wasn't happy.

"What are we doing in here?" he complained. "I'm allergic to evergreens. They make me sneeze and break out."

"We've got a great view of the car from here," Sabrina explained. "Besides, we need to talk."

Osgood sneezed. "What about?"

"Do you think Blair followed us to the cliff in that car?" Sabrina asked.

"Absolutely," Oz declared. "Let's ring the doorbell and arrest her."

"Don't be silly, Oz," Sabrina cautioned. "We need evidence for that."

"What about me?" Will protested. "I'm evidence! I saw her get into the car."

"Yes, but that doesn't prove that she drove to Lovers' Leap, or rammed our car. All we know for certain is that she was probably lying about meeting Charles at the train."

"Hey, look!" Oz whispered.

Jodi Biggs came out of the front door and down the sidewalk. She fiddled in her bag for a few moments, then got into the green Volvo and drove away.

"That's *Jodi's* car?" Osgood gasped as they stumbled out of the bushes. "I didn't even know she had a car."

"Will?" Sabrina asked. "Could you have been confused about who got into that car the night of the dance?"

"I *thought* it was Blair..." Suddenly Will seemed very unsure of himself. "Of course, it was really dark in the parking lot."

"If it was Jodi who killed Matt," Osgood said, "what was her motive?"

"She was really angry when Matt wouldn't dance with her," Sabrina said. "And I'm certain she knows I saw her take the money out of the cashbox."

"She was afraid you'd tell! So she followed you and Matt to Lovers' Leap and, in her drunken fury, killed the both of you!" Osgood was almost jumping up and down.

"That's not quite right, Oz." Sabrina shook her head in dismay. "I'm still alive."

"But I'm not."

At the sound of Matt's voice, Sabrina turned to see him standing near the kerb.

"Follow that car!" he directed.

CHAPTER THIRTEEN

"Where's Matt?" Osgood asked Sabrina as they cruised the streets of Innisfree, looking for Jodi. They were riding in the car that belonged to Sabrina's father. Will Stegeman had bailed out of the investigation because his parents expected him home. Matt had materialized for just a second, when they were at Blair's house, then vanished.

"He's probably here with us and just not letting us see him," Sabrina replied. She glanced in the rear-view mirror, hoping to catch sight of Matt's reflection. But he didn't appear.

"Well, I wish he'd say something," Osgood said, slumping against the window glass. "We've circled the mall and Main Street so many times I'm getting carsick."

"I don't know where else to look for her," Sabrina replied. "Think, Osgood! Where do kids round here go on a Saturday night?"

"You're asking me? The dateless wonder? I

never go out."

At the next intersection, Sabrina turned away from town and headed towards the park. It was one of the places she liked to go, to be by herself. Of course, that was during the day. Sabrina slowed the car as they passed the duck pond and the Japanese gardens.

"There she is!" Osgood pointed towards a girl weaving slightly as she made her way down the sidewalk at the edge of the kids' playground. "Pull over."

Sabrina slowed the car and eased over to the side of the road. Osgood rolled down the window. "Hi, Jodi," he called. "Need a ride?"

Jodi jerked her head up and blinked several times at Osgood. "Sure. Where are you headed?"

"Lovers' Leap," Sabrina shouted across Osgood.

"You two? So why do you want me to go with you?" Jodi sounded cautious. "That sounds bizarre."

Osgood turned to Sabrina and murmured, "Don't you think that's a little unsubtle?"

"No, I don't," she hissed back. "I think she needs to be hit over the head with the obvious." Sabrina stopped the engine and hopped out of the car. Then she hurried over to where Jodi was standing on the sidewalk, a confused look on her face.

"Jodi, I think you know what happened to Matt and me the night of the dance," Sabrina said bluntly. "I want you to return to the scene of the crime."

Jodi knitted her eyebrows, trying to comprehend what Sabrina was saying. "Everybody knows what happened that night. Matt was killed."

Osgood got out of the car and moved to Jodi's other side. "Confess, Jodi. Sabrina saw you steal money from the cashbox at the dance."

"Why would I do that?" Jodi staggered backwards and sat down heavily on to a park bench at the edge of the sidewalk. "I have money of my own."

"Yeah, shoplifting money," Sabrina said. "I saw you steal that clock from DrugFair and return it for a refund."

"You did?" Jodi's eyes widened.

"I know why you steal," Sabrina continued. "And why you're always out of money. Because you drink."

Osgood nodded. "Everyone knows about

your drinking problem."

Jodi's chin was starting to quiver. "What do you mean, everybody knows?"

Sabrina didn't let up. "You were angry at Matt for not dancing with you at the gym."

"Yes, I was – but I didn't kill him." Jodi had begun to sob with little hiccuping noises. She wiped at her nose with the back of her hand. "At least I don't think I did." Jodi dug in her bag for a tissue.

"Watch out for razor blades." Sabrina couldn't resist being sarcastic.

"What do you mean?" Jodi asked, finding an old tissue and blowing her nose hard. Sabrina could see a small bottle of vodka tucked into the side of her bag.

Osgood jumped in. "Where did you go after you left the dance?"

Sabrina put her hand on Jodi's bag. She was ready to wrestle the bottle away from her if necessary. "Tell us!"

"I don't know," Jodi confessed. "I drank most of a pretty big bottle of peppermint schnapps and couldn't walk. I passed out on the football field on the grass. The sirens woke me when the ambulances were on their way to Lovers' Leap the next morning." Jodi burst into tears again.

Her answer surprised both Sabrina and Osgood.

"The football field?" Osgood repeated. "All night? Did someone else have your car that night?"

"I don't know." Jodi shook her head repeatedly. "It was at my house when I got home. But I know I drove it to the gym the night before." Jodi covered her face with her hands.

"Maybe Will was right," Sabrina said to Osgood. "Maybe he really did see Blair get in Jodi's Volvo."

Osgood scratched his head. "But why would Blair take Jodi's car and not her own?"

Sabrina put her hand to her mouth. "Maybe she wanted to make it look like Jodi did it."

"But how could she drive the car, unless Jodi gave her the keys?"

Jodi, who was examining her Kleenex to find a part of it that wasn't used, murmured, "I always leave my keys in the car so I won't lose them. I figure it's so old, nobody would want to steal it. And I don't lock it."

"Then Blair could have used Jodi's car to push you two over the cliff." Osgood leapt to his feet and started pacing back and forth in front of the bench. "That way if anyone saw the

163

car, they would think Jodi was the murderer."

"And she probably figured that Jodi was so drunk," Sabrina joined in excitely, "she'd never remember if she did it or not."

What they were saying finally got through to Jodi, who raised her head and shouted, "You mean Blair murdered Matt and is trying to pin it on me?"

Sabrina and Osgood exchanged looks, and nodded. "Yes."

"I don't believe it! How could anybody kill Matt? Everyone loved Matt. He was the best friend, the nicest, most wonderful—" Jodi suddenly put her hand to her mouth. "I think I'm going to be sick."

Sabrina led Jodi to the park's drinking fountain and splashed some water on her face. "Blair's a monster," Jodi muttered. "I used to think she was my friend. I even got her into Stanford."

"Stanford?" Osgood jumped in. "How could you do that?"

"By switching the SAT tests," Jodi replied. "Her grades weren't good enough so I also made sure she got an A in history, even though she was failing it. I got her into the honour society, and—"

Osgood put his hands on Jodi's shoulders and stopped her talking. "You switched the SAT tests?"

"Yes," she told Oz. "I sneaked into the principal's office, after you'd finished taking the test, and erased your name on your test and wrote in hers, and vice versa."

An image flashed in Sabrina's head. It was from her first day of school when the test scores were announced. She remembered seeing a blonde – Jodi – run out of the principal's office and whisper to Blair, who'd seemed ecstatic. Jodi must have been breaking the news that her switch had worked.

"Switched the tests?" Osgood suddenly shrieked. "That's wonderful! That's fantastic!" He was so happy, he grabbed Jodi and kissed her on the lips. "Don't you see? I'm OK. I can cut it. I don't need to have them retest everyone!"

Jodi was startled by Osgood's kiss, but continued her confession. "Blair was really upset about your campaign to make the school give the test over again. She ordered me to get you to stop it."

"Wait a minute, Jodi," Sabrina cut in. "How can Blair give you orders?"

Jodi looked down at her bag, embarrassed. "Blair threatened to tell my parents that I drink. She said she could get me kicked off the cheerleading squad. I couldn't handle that." Jodi raised her head, a cunning smile on her face. "But I know Blair's secret."

"You do?" Sabrina expected Jodi to say that Blair had pushed Osgood's car off the cliff.

"Blair's totally in love with Charles York," Jodi explained. "I mean she's obsessed about him. She'd do anything to be with him. That's why she had me switch the SAT tests so she could be at Stanford with Charles."

"I've got news for Blair," Osgood said with a smirk. "Charles has a girlfriend at Stanford."

"He does? Really?" Oz nodded and Jodi suddenly began to laugh. "That's going to ruin all her plans. She'll end up at Stanford and Charles won't even know she's there!" Her laughter turned to hysterical sobbing, and she covered her face with her hands. "Oh, god. I can't believe she'd murder Matt. Oh my god."

Sabrina looped her arm over Jodi's shoulder and led her to the car. "Come on, Jodi, we'll take you home."

When they reached her house, Sabrina and Osgood helped Jodi to her front door. Sabrina gave her a quick hug and said, "Jodi, after you sleep this off, I think you should talk to your parents. They can probably help you work through this."

Jodi shrugged miserably. "I doubt it," she murmured, "But thanks, anyway."

As soon as they got back in the car, Oz collapsed with his head back against the seat. "Boy, that was painful."

Sabrina nodded. "Poor Jodi. She probably didn't realize how bad her drinking problem had got until it was too late to stop herself."

Osgood peered over his glasses at Sabrina. "So now we've got some good news and bad news. The good news is that I'm not an idiot, and Jodi is not a murderer. I've always kind of liked her, you know."

"So what's the bad news?"

"We still don't know who the murderer is," Osgood replied. "Blair might have taken Jodi's car, planning to murder Matt and pin it on Jodi. But why? Where's the motive?"

Sabrina sighed. "Good question. I wish Matt were here. He could probably help us sort this out."

"I heard everything."

Sabrina looked in the rear-view mirror and

saw Matt sitting in the back seat.

"Then why didn't you help us talk to Jodi?" Sabrina pulled the car over to the kerb and turned to look at him.

"Because you were doing great on your own! Magnificent! Breathtaking!" He grinned and she couldn't help but return it.

"Is he here?" Osgood was looking back over the seat, but couldn't see anything. Sabrina reached over and touched his arm with her unbandaged hand so that he could talk with Matt, too.

"That's a better picture," Osgood said as Matt appeared in his vision. "Thanks."

"So let's see what we've got," Matt said. "Blair is our most likely suspect. But we still don't have a motive."

"Jeff's back in the running, too," Sabrina added. "He could have rammed the car with his truck because he didn't want us to tell Heather about Mandy."

"That's true," Matt nodded. "That guy is—

"Pond scum," all three of them said at once.

Matt grinned at the two of them. "Great minds..."

Osgood shoved his glasses up on his nose. "Jeff may not be a mental giant but it's hard for me to imagine him killing someone to keep them quiet about his extra-curricular activities. I mean, he was at Lovers' Leap. What if other cars had gone there that night? Would he have shoved them all off the cliff?"

Matt cocked his head. "That's a good point. But if it wasn't Jeff, that brings us back to Blair. And we still don't have a motive."

Sabrina raised one finger. "I have an idea. I'll slip Blair a note saying that I remember everything that happened that night, and I want her to meet me somewhere to talk about it."

"Then what do we do?" Osgood asked.

"We recreate the scene of the crime and she'll be so freaked out – she'll confess everything!"

Osgood grinned. "I like it. It's simple, to the point, and sounds like something out of a Hitchcock movie."

Matt wasn't quite so certain. "I think we can pull off the freaking her out bit, but Blair's pretty tough. Not like Jodi. I'm not sure she'll break so easily."

"Oh, yes, she will." Sabrina set her mouth stubbornly. "Because I'm going to make her!"

CHAPTER FOURTEEN

Neptune is trine the transiting Moon today.
The eyes have it: look, and then look again.
The solution to a problem is in something you
see, not something you touch or feel. See it in
your mind. Reason it out.

Fog was beginning to roll into the low-lying areas of Innisfree when Sabrina steered her car into a side road. She could barely see a few metres in front of her as she moved along at a slow pace, looking for the sign. Finally her headlights landed on a rusty tin building with a large loading door. STEGEMAN'S AUTO SHOP was painted on the side.

The building was at a dead end in the industrial part of town which was filled with warehouses and yards loaded with freshly cut lumber. Empty railroad tracks cut through the area, but there were no trains. No people. No activity. Not tonight.

It certainly is creepy here.

It was decided the meeting with Blair should take place at Stegeman's. Will had suggested it, since he had extra keys to his father's garage and was now in on the plan. He was, in fact, a valuable part of it. The plan was to recreate the events of that fateful night and force Blair's hand.

Osgood and Will were to go to the waterworks, where they knew Blair would be holding court at the Atomic Café, and hand her the note from Sabrina, which said that she remembered everything and wanted Blair to meet her at Stegeman's. Then they were to follow Blair to make sure she went to the meeting.

The plan was to make the garage seem deserted, and it was. Sabrina parked her car and hurried towards the darkened garage. The fog was thick, but there was a moon. It looked like a flashlight shining through thick gauze, and provided a little illumination.

For once, she'd dressed like most of the girls in Innisfree – jeans, a sweatshirt and sneakers. It was a practical choice, considering what she might have to do tonight.

Sabrina felt with her fingers along the tin

siding until she located the door handle, and rattled it slightly. It slid open a tiny bit and she wondered if she should go in.

Sabrina stuck her head inside. "Hello? Is anybody here?"

She opened the door some more, enough to slip into the shop, and closed it behind her. Will had found another Buick, nearly identical to Osgood's old one, and parked it in the garage. When her eyes adjusted to the darkness, Sabrina spotted the vehicle at the far end of the building. She hurried across the concrete floor and got into the car, on the passenger's side.

"Matt?" she whispered. "If I ever needed you, I need you now."

"That's good to hear." Matt materialized behind the wheel on the driver's side, exactly where he'd been on the night of the accident. "Don't worry. I'm right beside you."

"I wish Osgood or Will were here. Why did we think it was a good idea to have me be here alone?"

"You're not alone. I'm here, remember?" Matt murmured. "But they both needed to be at the Waterworks to be sure that Blair left. If she hadn't responded to plan A, Will was going to remove her distributor cap and then have her

172

car towed to the garage."

Sabrina hadn't expected the garage to be so creepy, and that's what was disturbing her. The dark corners were filled with eerie shadows thrown by the tools used by the mechanics. The compressed-air hoses dangling from a grid in the ceiling looked like twisted vines in the half-light. Only a dim glow coming from the moon filtered through the grease-caked windows.

"What if Blair gets here before the guys do?"

"Shh!" Matt whispered. "I hear something."

Sabrina listened to the door to the garage rattle, then open and shut. She heard footsteps and then silence.

She turned in the seat. She wasn't able to see anything, not even Matt, but still she whispered, "What do I do now?"

Click!

Two shop lights at the far end of the garage came on. They were pointed at the rear of the old car where Sabrina was waiting. Suddenly she was illuminated, but she couldn't see who had turned on the lights because of the terrible glare.

Will had deliberately set the lights so they would shine on the car but she hadn't counted on them being so powerful. They made her eyes water.

173

"Hello? Who's there?" Sabrina put her head out of the car window and yelled. There was no immediate answer.

At the other end of the garage, behind the lights, Blair stood speechless. She had flipped on a light switch by the door and was now looking at the car parked at the end of the garage. She gasped in recognition.

"Sabrina?" Blair took a few uneasy steps towards the vehicle. "Is that you?"

"Yes," Sabrina replied. "In Osgood's car."

"Don't be ridiculous. Osgood's car was totalled," Blair said, in an irritated but shaky voice. "Why are you doing this? First I get a note saying you know everything and now this silly charade."

"I need your help, Blair," Sabrina said, getting out of the car. "I'm trying to catch Matt's murderer."

"Murderer? There was no murder. The police said it was an accident. The brakes gave out."

"But I remember that we were pushed. Over that cliff."

"Pushed?" Blair repeated, carefully. "Who pushed you?"

"The headlights blinded me a bit and I couldn't see who was driving, but I'm sure

174

about the car. Do you know anyone with a green Volvo?"

"Of course I do – Jodi Biggs. So why don't you tell the police this story?"

"Because of another memory I have," Sabrina bluffed. "Of Jodi passed out cold on the football field. Now how could Jodi have driven all the way to Lovers' Leap if she was passed out at the high school?"

"How should I know?" Blair looked nervously over her shoulder at the door to the garage. "She drives drunk all the time." Blair checked her watch. "Look, I've really got to go. I don't know why you asked me to meet you here—"

"Better get to the point," Matt urged. "She's going to leave the garage."

"Where were you the night Matt was murdered?" Sabrina demanded.

Blair met the challenge evenly. "I was at the train station meeting my boyfriend, Charles."

"Boyfriend?" Sabrina folded her arms across her chest. "That's news. I heard Charles has a different girlfriend. From Stanford."

"What?" Blair was taken totally by surprise. "Where'd you hear that?"

"So I doubt very much that you were meeting

Charles, when that very weekend he brought his fiancée home to meet his parents."

"Fiancée!" Blair screeched. Her whole demeanor changed. She narrowed her eyes and advanced on Sabrina. "You're making this up. Just to upset me. It won't work."

"It's working like gangbusters," Matt whispered. "But be careful, Sabrina, I don't like the look in her eye."

"What were you two doing in Osgood's car that night, anyway?" Blair suddenly demanded.

This question confused Sabrina. "What do you mean, what were we doing in Osgood's car?"

"Matt always drove that little red car."

"It was in the garage," Sabrina replied.

"What's she getting at?" Matt rumbled.

"Osgood was the only person that ever drove that junk heap," Blair muttered, almost to herself.

"Oh, my god," Matt suddenly cried. "Now I get it."

"What?" Sabrina forgot Blair was there and turned to Matt.

"She was trying to kill Osgood, not me. It was all a mistake."

Sabrina turned back to Blair. "You were

trying to murder *Osgood*? Why?"

Matt answered for Blair. "Because of the SAT test." Matt put his hand to his head and spun in a circle, moaning. "A stupid test!"

Sabrina faced Blair, horrified. "Jodi switched the tests and you got an extremely high score. High enough to get you into Stanford. And everything would have been fine if Osgood hadn't made such a fuss about the scores."

Blair listened to Sabrina, stony-faced. She neither confirmed nor denied what Sabrina was saying.

"Then at the dance that night Osgood issued the Osgood Challenge, saying he planned to go to the principal and demand that the whole school be retested." Sabrina was quickly putting the pieces together. "You couldn't take it. You followed his car out of the parking lot, planning to do something – anything – to make him stop. When you saw his car go to Lovers' Leap, you had the perfect opportunity to get rid of him."

"I never wanted to kill anyone," Blair said, moving slowly towards the workbench. "I wanted to warn Osgood to stop it. That's all."

"But when you hit the car, Jodi's Volvo was strong enough to push that old Buick over the cliff," Sabrina finished.

"It was an accident," Blair said, her nostrils flaring. "An accident!"

"Tell that to the police," Sabrina hissed. Suddenly all of the anger and sorrow welled up inside Sabrina. She exploded at Blair. "How could you be so stupid? You murdered Matt and ruined all of our lives."

"It wasn't murder," Blair shouted back. "I told you, it was an accident."

"An accident? This is too absurd to be true," Matt cried. He was in a frenzy. "I died because this person wanted to go to Stanford! It's all one big joke on me!"

In wanting to comfort Matt, Sabrina turned her attention away from Blair. Just long enough for Blair to grab a compressed-air stapler from the workbench. She aimed it at Sabrina and a stream of metal staples flew at her like bullets. One grazed her leg and Sabrina screamed in pain.

"Matt, help me!" Sabrina covered her face to protect her eyes from the sharp missiles and ran for cover.

"Matt can't help you now." Blair moved closer and fired another round. "You wouldn't be warned - I tried with the bench at the café, then again with the razor blades, but this time

I've got you!"

"Ow!" A staple stabbed into Sabrina's neck and her hand flew to it. She knew she was bleeding.

"Grab her arm, Sabrina," Matt yelled.

"Grab her? I've got to get away from her!" Sabrina screamed back.

"Just do it!"

Sabrina made a dive for Blair and caught her arm.

"Let go of me!" Blair screamed as she struggled to point the staple gun at Sabrina. Then she froze wide-eyed at the sight of the terrifying spectre hovering in front of her.

"You murdered me," Matt howled, raising his arms above his head in his best ghost imitation. "And now I'm coming to get you!"

Blair let out a blood-curdling scream. Sabrina took advantage of Blair's panic to wrest the staple gun out of her hands. Then Blair turned and bolted towards the door.

"No, you don't!" Sabrina tackled her halfway across the room. Pain shot though her injured hand and ankle, but Sabrina was not about to let go. Not with victory so near. "Do something, Matt!"

Matt put his face close to Blair's. "You

thought you could get rid of me," he intoned. "But now I'm going to haunt you for the rest of your life."

Blair's eyes rolled back in her head and for just a second, Sabrina thought she was going to faint. Instead she scrambled to her feet.

"You can run," Matt roared after Blair as she stumbled for the big metal sliding door. "But you can't hide. From me, or yourself."

Blair pulled back the door and found herself face to face with Osgood and Will.

"She's trying to get away," Sabrina rasped, pulling herself to her feet. "Stop her."

Osgood caught Blair first, shouting, "She's tricky. Before she left the waterworks, she punctured the tyres on Dad's car."

Will grabbed Blair's other arm, adding, "We had to walk here."

"Let go of me! My father will sue you!" Blair was kicking and screaming but the boys held on.

"She was trying to get *you*, Osgood," Sabrina cried. "She thought it was *you* in the Buick."

"Get me?" Osgood looked down at Blair in surprise. "But why?"

"The test scores," Sabrina answered.

Blair wouldn't stop kicking but the two boys

180

managed to get her hands behind her back. Then Will wrapped his bicycle lock chain round her hands and padlocked her to the big sliding door.

"There!" he said with a proud smile. "I'm making a citizen's arrest!"

"Good work, Will." Osgood was still holding Blair fast and she sunk her teeth into his arm. "Ouch! She bit me!" Osgood was amazed.

"I'm going to do a lot more than that if you don't let me go!" Blair hissed.

"Oh, like what? Kill me?" Osgood leant forward and whispered right into her face, "Goodbye, Stanford."

Blair spat at him.

As the boys led Blair out of the shop, Sabrina held her hand over her neck where the staple had wounded her and said, "Well, we didn't exactly get a confession of murder but I'd say trying to kill me with that staple gun is the next best thing. What do you think, Matt?"

There was no reply.

"Matt?" Sabrina spun in a circle, peering into the dark recesses of the garage. "Matt, I can't see you any more! Matt, are you there? Matt?"

It wasn't just the silence, it was a feeling deep inside Sabrina that told her Matt was gone.

CHAPTER FIFTEEN

Mercury in retrograde has thrown you into a melancholy quandary, Scorpio. At long last, you've found something, or someone, to love – but you can't keep it. Remember, all losses aren't bad – they just "are". As the song says, "If you love somebody – set them free". The heart you free may be your own.

*T*he large tree in the cemetery was bare of leaves and winter was in full force in the village of Innisfree. Snow had already blanketed the town.

Sabrina pulled the collar of her leather jacket up round her neck for warmth and sat down on the few remaining leaves that lingered beneath the old oak tree. She didn't care if she got her coveralls dirty since they were already covered in paint. Sabrina had decided to repaint her room from grey to a bright colour – yellow! She had thrown herself into the project in order to lift her spirits.

She breathed a heavy sigh, then leant back against the trunk and closed her eyes.

It's hard to believe it's all over. Will my life ever be normal again? And what is normal?

In the past few months, Blair had been remanded to the authorities. She was charged with murder and held in jail, without bail. It had been a scandal for her family and the town had been swarming with reporters.

The local news was that Heather and Jeff had got back together. This time Heather was sporting a new ring with a very small stone. Jeff called it a peace offering. Heather called it an engagement ring.

Jodi had talked to her parents about her problem and was now attending local Alcoholics Anonymous meetings for teens. She seemed truly grateful for the help she was getting and had actually thanked Sabrina for making her face up to her problem.

Osgood had happily regained his title as genius of the universe and had his high SAT scores to prove it. A college scholarship was forthcoming.

Sabrina had recently been getting a taste of what her normal life was going to be. She had joined the staff at the newspaper, writing a bi-weekly column on the arts and things to do in the Northern California area.

She liked the newspaper job and had made some new friends. Of course, Sabrina felt she'd always be closer to Osgood and Will than anybody, since theirs was a bond forged out of truly extraordinary circumstances. They were already a threesome, spending many long hours watching *Jeopardy* at Osgood's house, learning basic car repairs with Will, and exploring the art galleries of northern California with Sabrina.

Sabrina hadn't seen Matt since the night at the garage when Blair's involvement had become clear. It seemed he had been back on earth just long enough to find out who had killed him.

Though Sabrina spent a good deal of her time thinking about Matt, it wasn't until today that she was filled with such an strong need to see him again.

It had hit her in the middle of painting her room. Instead of the smell of wet paint, her bedroom and the whole house was inexplicably filled with the scent of roses. Sabrina had dropped her brush and raced into the hall, half-expecting to see her mother there smiling at her. Once in the hall she could hear her father typing away furiously in his study. He was nearing the final chapter and had often been in tears, knowing he was about to put the love story to rest.

The sweet aroma of roses was as strong in her father's study as it was in her room. She stuck her head through the door to speak to him, but paused. He was chuckling to himself as he typed.

He must be remembering some wonderful moment with Mother. I won't interrupt him.

Thoughts of her mother made Sabrina think of Matt. Two spirits no longer part of her world. Suddenly Sabrina was overcome by the urge to see Matt. Without hesitation, she marched to the front closet, threw on her jacket, and ran out of the house. Before she knew it she was standing under "their" oak tree at the cemetery, looking out at the view.

The gingerbread houses, the mountains that ran right down into the sea, the mysterious fog...those were the things her mother had loved about this place, too. Fate had brought Sabrina to Innisfree, and she felt it was all part of a larger picture she hoped to understand some day.

"How does that poem go?" Sabrina closed

her eyes and murmured, "I will arise and go now."

"And go to Innisfree," a voice whispered. And once again Sabrina smelled the delicious scent of roses.

"Mother," Sabrina breathed softly. She was afraid to frighten her spirit away.

"And a small cabin build there, of clay and
  wattles made.
Nine bean rows will I have there, a hive for
  the honey-bee,
And live alone in the bee-loud glade."

Her mother's face appeared in Sabrina's head, the familiar little smile lines crinkling round her eyes. Her face was full of love and peace.

Her mother nodded and continued the poem.

"And I shall have some peace there, for
  peace comes dropping slow,
Dropping from veils of the morning to where
  the cricket sings;
There midnight's all a glimmer, and noon a
  purple glow,
And evening full of the linnet's wings."

Sabrina listened to her mother's voice and was filled full of love as tangible as warm honey.

"I will arise and go now, for always night
   and day
I hear lake water lapping with low sounds by
   the shore;
While I stand on the roadway, or on the
   pavements grey,
I hear it in the deep heart's core."

When the poem was finished, Sabrina kept her eyes closed, savouring the moment. Then a gentle breeze brushed her fringe off her forehead as her mother had done so many times when she was a child going to sleep.

"Excuse me," a voice called from behind Sabrina.

Sabrina slowly opened her eyes. A dark-haired boy stood on the road that circled the cemetery. He had a large golden retriever on a leash. The dog wagged its tail at Sabrina.

"I don't mean to intrude," the boy said walking towards Sabrina. "But I'm new here—"

"And you're lost?" Sabrina asked.

"Who, me, lost?" the boy joked. "Never! Actually, I was just trying to get a feel for the place."

His words sounded strangely familiar. "Checking the vibes?" she said, remembering a conversation she'd had her first day of school.

The boy grinned a crooked smile. "You might say that."

As he drew closer, Sabrina could see the colour of his eyes – pale blue, with little gold flecks highlighting them. So much like Matt's, they startled her.

He seemed to have the same surprised expression on his face as he looked into her eyes. They held each other's gaze for a few moments. Then he said, "Have we met before?"

A slow smile spread across Sabina's face. "It's possible."

"It's very odd." The boy's eyes were still locked with hers. "I was out walking my dog and suddenly I was here. It feels sort of like—"

"Fate," Sabrina said with him. "I know."

The boy continued to study her face. "Would you like to take a walk?" he asked. "Get better acquainted?"

Sabrina glanced over her shoulder towards Matt's grave, and back at the boy. "I'd love to."

The afternoon breeze, carrying the faint scent of roses, caressed her cheek as they walked together down the hill.

*ARIES*TAURUS*GEMINI*CANCER*LEO*VIRGO*LIBRA*
*SCORPIO*SAGITTARIUS*CAPRICORN*AQUARIUS*PISCES*

Twelve signs of the Zodiac. Twelve novels, each one embracing the characteristics of a zodiac sign. Pushed to the extreme, these characteristics lead down twisting paths into tales of mystery, horror, romance and fantasy.

Whatever your sun sign, you will want to read Zodiac, the series written in the stars.

ARIES	SECRET IDENTITY
TAURUS	BLACK OUT
GEMINI	MIRROR IMAGE
CANCER	DARK SHADOWS
LEO	STAGE FRIGHT
VIRGO	DESPERATELY YOURS
LIBRA	FROZEN IN TIME
SCORPIO	DEATH GRIP
SAGITTARIUS	STRANGE DESTINY
CAPRICORN	DON'T LOOK BACK
AQUARIUS	SECOND SIGHT
PISCES	SIXTH SENSE

SERIES CREATED BY JAHNNA N. MALCOLM

PISCES:
A DREAMER, KNOWS SECRETS
SIXTH SENSE

*P*hoebe is a loner. She can sense when something's wrong, but people distrust her and are afraid of her premonitions. When Mark Chenier disappears, images grow in Phoebe's mind – she knows where Mark is, but no one, except her Cajun grandmother, believes her. Can she prove that she is right and that her 'dreams' really tell the truth?

CANCER:
EMOTIONAL, CARING
DARK SHADOWS

*C*hloe works tirelessly in her garden to create something beautiful, but nothing seems to flourish. Is it because a murderer used to live in the house before Chloe and her brother moved in? Then, a secret helper transforms the garden overnight – a secret helper who doesn't want Chloe to know his identity. Can the murder and the secret gardener be linked and can caring Chloe put the pieces of the chain together?

CAPRICORN:
PERSISTENT, AN ACHIEVER
DON'T LOOK BACK

*C*at is terrified. Her nightmares have returned. The house with the tiny staircase and the door... the door that Cat never opens. But Cat is determined to conquer her fears, she has made new friends and she wants to keep them. Then one night at a slumber party she finds that door and her nightmares become reality as she remembers the terrifying secret of what happened beyond the door.

TAURUS:
PATIENT, PRACTICAL
BLACK OUT

*T*ess can't remember much. Except that the Halloween party went wrong. There was a fire and people were trapped. But it wasn't an accident. Tess knows who the murderer is – if only she could remember... Her patience is put to the test in a deadly waiting game.